Death is in the garden

Books by Melba Marlett

The dead woman looked strangely like Dolores Kennedy, only child of wealthy parents. But it was Dolores herself who stumbled over the body outside the exclusive Philadelphia girls' school she attended. And Inspector Davis could find nothing but coincidence to tie the two together.

It was this striking resemblance that kept Davis hunting odd facts and tracing peculiar clues for more than a year. During those months a man was tried for the murder and acquitted. Dolores became sunk in a deep lethargy, and her interest in life was aroused only by the appearance next door of a very eligible bachelor, a man whose suave manners and social competence were belied by his private behavior.

Dolores started by being curious about her neighbor, and ended by being deeply attracted to him. Their unusual relationship, plus the sudden appearance of an old flame of Dolores', brought this strange case to an unexpected climax—which Inspector Davis resolved almost by remote control.

BY MELBA MARLETT

Death is in the garden

WILDSIDE PRESS

All of the characters in this book are fictitious, and
any resemblance to actual persons, living or dead, is purely coincidental.

For Leo B. Grimes, my brother

Piteous little love,
Death is in the garden, time runs down,
The year that simple and unexalted ran till now
Ferments in winy autumn, and I must die.

FROM BLACK MARIGOLDS
11TH CENTURY, SANSKRIT
TRANSLATION BY E. POWYS MATHERS

1

The room had a simple opulence, an un-cluttered magnificence. Firelight danced on the pale blue draperies, brought out the plum tones in the deep crimson carpeting, flick-ered on silver and the high luster of Lenox vases, shone softly on brass paper knife and porcelain stamp box. The chairs were delicate affairs of gilt and needlepoint, straight-backed and armless orna-ments that had no intention of giving comfort to a weary spine. Even the desk had lost its functional lines and looked like a pretty painted toy, its gilt legs curled cautiously beneath it safe from the awkwardness of human beings.

Yet the meaning and purpose of the room lay locked within those desk drawers in folder after folder of photographs, all of girls. There were big, handsome portraits of serene young faces with hair flying or conventionally coifed or subdued beneath a bridal veil; there were snapshots of girls in bathing suits or riding habits or tennis shorts; there were pictures of young matrons proudly holding their babies for the dazzlement of the camera. And on all these were the messages inscribed by their givers: "To Miss Stone, with love," "In memory of the happiest days of my life," "To Miss Stone, with appreciation." Kathryn Stone, head-mistress of Stone Oaks, counted her years not by gray hairs or wrinkles, but by the number and variety of those photographs. Long ago the tide of them had burst the confines of the long, businesslike desk in her office, and she had removed them to this, her private sitting room. Occasionally, in a quiet evening, she would take them out, look at the faces, smile or frown to herself. Who would have thought that Marilyn Mosher—wild, careless little Marilyn—would take so kindly to wifehood and motherhood and a sedate social order? And Kitty Bryan had turned into a real beauty, as Kathryn Stone had always thought she would. And how shy, intelligent Mary Ann Myers had turned into the head of a very active advertising agency proved that one could never tell what kind of chicken would come out of an egg. Sometimes Miss Stone felt that she was the gratified great-aunt of most of the young women in the United States.

But at the moment she was not gratified. She was reading a story which one of her present students had written for English class, and as she turned the pages covered with gently slanting script—Stone Oaks girls were not encouraged to use typewriters, good penmanship was one of the marks of a lady—her patient mouth tightened with disapproval. As she finished, she gathered the pages in her slender hands and pushed them away as if they were not quite clean. There was danger in that manuscript. Danger to Miss Stone and to the school and, most of all, to Dolores Kennedy, who had written it. Sighing, rubbing her temples, Miss Stone wished for the thousandth time that she were omnipotent, that she could decide at once the proper thing to do. But her mind was a confusion of shadows: the trustees of the school, the mothers of her other girls, the parents of Dolores far off at their home on River Island. What would be right, what would be fair to all of them?

Miss Woods, the English mistress, came in, advancing purposefully to a chair by the fireplace. "You've read it, Kathryn?"

"Yes. I don't know what to think."

Miss Woods eased her considerable weight on to one of the little gilded chairs. "She may have been reading too much of the wrong kind of fiction, you know. The whole thing could be a flight of fancy."

"I doubt that, Sarah. And you doubt it, too, or you wouldn't have brought it to me."

"Honestly, you never know, do you? Of all our girls, I'd have said that Dolores Kennedy was the least likely to be—promiscuous."

Miss Stone uncrossed her slender legs and pushed a crystal cigarette box toward her colleague. "You're using the word in its broadest sense, of course. Actually, it's not that she's promiscuous, but that she knows one man too well." She rose and began to walk back and forth, studying the toe of each slipper as it swung into its forward arc. "Richard Jordan, I suppose."

"Richard Jordan, you hope."

"Cowardly of me, I know. But they've known each other all their lives, they're engaged, their families approve, and—if there are going to be repercussions—well, the situation could be worse."

"Still, she's our responsibility while she's here." Miss Woods smiled. "Being a spinster myself, I don't know what's usual in a long engagement. Perhaps nobody waits for the marriage ceremony any more and we're being a couple of old fuddy-duddies."

"We can't say 'God bless you' to an illicit affair even if it turns legal tomorrow." She ran a hand over her ash-blond hair. "I suppose the thing to do is get it over with."

"Going to call her in?"

Miss Stone paused, her hand on the house telephone. "Yes. How's the weather?"

"Regular November wind, little snow, not bad underfoot."

"Then I'll ask her to step over. She's in Alma House, fortunately."

She spoke briefly into the telephone, and Miss Woods got to her feet. "You'd rather I left, wouldn't you, Kathryn?"

"No, I'd rather you stayed, coward that I am. But I think it's best that you stay out of the unpleasantness of it. I don't want her resenting you and failing English in consequence."

"I brought her record card up from the office, in case you needed it. I'll leave it on the desk here."

"Thank you, Sarah."

She turned the card over in her hands. The marks were good, the teachers' comments flattering. "Capable girl." "A real flair for poetry." "Beautiful manners." These remarks were never shown to the girl under discussion, they were private signposts to point the way in an emergency. Miss Stone shook her head in bewilderment. What her faculty seemed to be trying to tell her was that Dolores Kennedy could simply not be guilty of a shabby amour. And against that theory sentences in the girl's own writing leaped into mind: "Even in his sleep, if she laid a hand on his arm, he would reach for it, tuck it against him, smiling, so deep was his awareness of her." "Beside such love as she felt for him, conventionality seemed a stiff, pale ghost, made of the paper on which gossiping acquaintances might write to each other." "Eighteen was the legal 'age of consent,' but twenty-one was the age when her parents would consent to her consenting. It had been a long time to wait. Too long."

A soft voice said, "You wanted to see me, Miss Stone?"

She had thought she knew Dolores very well, but she had had no occasion to notice her this term, and the change made her gasp. This was no girl, it was a young woman. There was poise beneath the softness and self-assurance under the well-bred reserve. Miss Stone's experienced nostrils flared a little, picking up the scent of maturity as an expert in scents detects the musk or ambergris under a flower odor.

"Yes. Come in, my dear."

"I didn't bother to dress. I hope you don't mind."

"Not at all. Shall I take your coat?"

Dolores smiled, shrugging the gray squirrel from her shoulders. "It's wet a little. And my hair has some snow on it too."

"We'll put you both by the fire to dry out."

The purple velvet of the girl's housecoat swept the crimson carpet, triumphed over it. It fell in elegant, graceful folds as she sat down in the indicated chair, and its highlights gave a bluish sheen to her black hair, a purple depth to her deep blue eyes. She did not cross her knees. She sat, effortlessly erect, hands as fragile and curling as magnolia flowers resting easily in her lap. Miss Stone felt a sudden embarrassment. How could she bring herself to play prying old woman to this lovely, self-contained creature?

"The house mistress said you wanted to talk to me about something important."

Miss Stone summoned her forces. "It's about the story you turned in to Miss Woods."

14

The girl's eyelashes swept upward in surprise. "Wasn't it any good, Miss Stone? I thought it was the best thing I'd done."

"I'm sure that it has artistic merit, but—frankly—we found the subject matter disturbing." Miss Stone smiled bravely. "Miss Woods thought that you might have patterned it after something you had read, but there's a strong sense of actual experience under-lying it that—well, that left me a little breathless."

Was there a deepening of color on the girl's face? Her eyes were steady enough. "I'm not sure I understand just what you mean, Miss Stone."

"It isn't easy to be plain about an intimate part of someone else's life. Believe me, if you had not been placed in my charge by your parents, I wouldn't dream of mentioning the matter. A woman's love affairs should certainly be her own province and within the domain of her own discretion and conscience."

"I see. You think I'm having a love affair." Dolores smiled happily. "I suppose I am."

"I shall have to ask you to explain that," said Miss Stone steadily.

"It's nothing that I mind explaining. I'm to be married next summer sometime, after I've finished here and Richard is through at the university, and I've been in love with him since I was ten. Is that what you wanted to know?"

"Richard is the only young man with whom you go out?"

"I've gone out with other men, but only because my father insisted. Richard was the only one I ever *wanted* to go out with."

"Your father was wise. A too-early concentration on a member of the opposite sex is unhealthy. In my position, I've seen the bad results of it a good many times."

Dolores smiled shyly, beautifully. "Dad gave up when I turned twenty. For the last year I've been dating only Richard. Mother says I may have my ring in June, when the engagement will be formally announced. We're to be married in August."

The girl's serenity was reassuring. Here, as Miss Stone had hoped, was no fly-by-night affair, but an arrangement that had a parental blessing. Looking at the demure figure in purple velvet, the acme of propriety, the flower of Stone Oaks teaching, the headmistress began to feel much happier. Impossible to believe that this girl, sheltered and well-bred, should have been gaining pre-nuptial experience in the only places where such learning was possible: parked cars, hotel rooms, the houses of sophisticated and complacent friends. Still, there was the story Dolores had written. Still, there was the deplorable fact that Miss Stone was anxious to believe that nothing was wrong. Optimism was often merely an indisposition to face unpleasant truths, and Miss Stone scolded herself for feeling confident too soon.

She picked up the card with the girl's record on it. "I see that you have been granted leave the past three week ends to visit your uncle in New York."

Dolores shifted in her chair, stretched a satin toe to the fire. "Yes. Uncle Winthrop Canby. He's been ill, poor dear."

Winthrop Canby. Winthrop Canby. The name sounded familiar, and it tolled itself over and over in Miss Stone's mind with no significance except a sour overtone that was as inexplicable as the faint familiarity of the name.

"Your uncle makes his home in New York City?"

"He has several homes. Mother and I visited him at his Florida house once. But this is an apartment on Riverside Drive." She looked back appealingly over her half-averted shoulder. "I've asked permission to go again this week end. Mrs. Rhodes hasn't told me yet if I might be allowed."

All the antennae of her intuition trembling, Miss Stone studied the card. Dolores had been on campus steadily since the beginning of the term in September except for the week end of the Junior-Senior Prom at Eastern U and these last three week ends. The prom week end was not momentous. Several of the girls had been invited, and the lot of them had progressed to the university under competent chaperonage (although Miss Stone made a mental note about checking with Miss Barrow, the chaperon of that past expedition, at once). But these last three week ends were unknown quantities. Was Mr. Canby a proper person to have charge of an impressionable young niece? And there was always the horrible possibility that this lovely young lady might be falsifying her true whereabouts and had not gone to New York at all. Dear God, prayed Miss Stone, don't let her be as bad as all that.

"Naturally, we can't have you away every week end," said Miss Stone gently.

Dolores turned toward her, dismayed. "He really is very sick, Miss Stone. It's his gall bladder, and, if he doesn't improve soon, they're going to have to operate. He's an old man, and the idea terrifies him. He isn't married—he's a woman-hater, you know—and he won't tell Mother, because he says that sisters ought not to be allowed in sickrooms, they're too bossy. So, really, all he has is myself."

"I'm afraid that he's putting too great a responsibility on you, Dolores. If he's as ill as you say, his family should be notified."

The girl gave a little cry of protest. "Does that mean I can't go there any more, Miss Stone?"

Yes, something wrong here. Something decidedly wrong. "I haven't said that. I'll consult with your house mother and you'll know tomorrow." She smiled at the girl's distraught face. "This isn't helping us much about your paper, is it?"

"I shouldn't have written that story. I knew it the moment I'd turned it in. It was all imagination, but I shouldn't have chosen a plot like that. Perhaps I was trying to be clever, or perhaps I didn't think at all." She threw out an imploring hand. "I'll apologize to Miss Woods. I'll apologize to you. I'll do anything if only——"

The passionate voice stopped suddenly, and Miss Stone finished the sentence to herself, "If only you'll let me go to New York." That was what the girl had meant, had stopped barely short of saying.

"My dear," she said gravely, "you must see that you are making me more suspicious of your motives by this emotional display. A young woman doesn't get so aroused over an invalid uncle. Will you be quite frank with me? Will you tell me what there is about these trips to New York that makes them so very important to you?"

"There's nothing to tell." Her face was controlled now, eyes downcast, mouth calm. Only her voice betrayed the excitement within. Though she pitched it low, she could not suppress the quiver in it. "I've told you everything."

Miss Stone rose brightly. "Then I mustn't detain you any longer. Mrs. Rhodes will tell you our decision in the morning."

"Thank you, Miss Stone."

Ah, the blessedness of social convention and good manners. By their grace, these two women, now adversaries, went through all the smiling motions of guest and hostess in farewell. The let-me-help-you's and the oh-don't-bother's and the inquiries about the possible amount of snow for tomorrow. Voices brave and carelessly cheerful. Eyes watchful above smiling lips. Miss Stone held her breath. If there could not be honesty between them, then let there be this decent entombment of their differences. As the girl moved toward the door, a sad composure on her face, her shoulders gently weary, Miss Stone laid a hand in accolade on the gray squirrel. Not many young women could feel so deeply and behave so decently at the same time.

But the touch was a mistake. It cracked the girl's reserve and whirled her about, made her clutch the kindly fingers, brought the white storm back into her face. "I'm doing nothing wrong, Miss Stone. Please, I'm not. I'm not breaking any rules or spoiling anyone's life. If I could make you understand! You see, I'm shy, I've always been rather—alone. I like the girls here, but they're not my friends. Oh, we wish each other well, but I don't have the gift of intimacy with people. Being an only child and so long away from home—you can't know what these little vacations with my uncle mean to me. Even though he isn't well, he's witty and clever. And the most fascinating people come to visit him, and I sit and listen to them talk and it's thrilling and exciting. Sometimes I feel as if I'd never been alive before. I couldn't bear to be deprived of it, Miss Stone. I'm willing to abide by regulations, but it would be uselessly cruel to deprive me of that!"

Miss Stone did not speak at once. She left a little space of quiet, her habit with emotional visitors, so that the girl might hear her own words beating on the air. The silence had its effect. It bled the fever away and left the girl pale and sane and conscious of her fault.

"Tell me," said Miss Stone at last, "does Richard Jordan also visit your uncle on these week ends?"

18

The dark head drooped against the gray fur. The voice was nearly inaudible. "Yes."

"Does he stay there? Live there?"

"No."

"He comes in from the university and takes a room somewhere in town?"

"I believe he stays at the Eastern Club."

"And he visits you from there?"

"Yes."

"Frequently?"

"Yes."

"Would you say that you go there to listen to all the fascinating people—or to see Richard Jordan?"

"Both."

"So you were not quite honest with me before?"

"I was—partly honest."

"If Mr. Jordan can go to New York to visit you, is there any reason why he could not visit you here?"

"There is no place here where we can be alone."

"And you feel the need of being alone with him?"

The pansy eyes came up at last, and, shockingly, they held a flicker of contempt. "What a strange question," said Dolores wonderingly.

Miss Stone hid the sting of the implied criticism. "I will take the matter under advisement, Dolores. I can tell you no more than that. We're old fogies, I know, but you must try to be patient with us. Good night."

She saw apology wavering to the girl's lips, but she smiled and closed the door on it. No more emotion tonight. She was exhausted by it already. What was needed now was cool reason.

"Miss Barrow, please," she said into the telephone.

As she sat listening to Miss Barrow's dry, sedate voice over the wire, she felt her nerves relax. Yes, Miss Barrow remembered the prom expedition. No, there had been absolutely no funny business about it. Dolores had stayed with the group, had shown no inclination to wander away on her own. She and her young man had been models of behavior, though, Miss Barrow might add, if ever she had seen a young man in love, Richard Jordan was it. "He's absolutely wild about her, Miss Stone, but he's very nice about it. None of this immodest demonstration in public. He may have kissed her good night—I always made it a point to be busy with the cabman or taking off my galoshes at that point—but it didn't go beyond that. My impression of Dolores is that she wouldn't have permitted any real laxity anyway. She's a tame sort of girl."

Miss Stone suppressed a smile. "Are you deploring that, Blanche?"

"No. I was thankful for it. But, off the record, I may say that I like girls with a little more—juice—to them. The reason Dolores likes Richard is that he's so gentle with her. I think she'd swoon if he were to make an active pass."

"Then it will relieve your feelings to learn that we suspect that he *has* made an active pass and that she has not swooned."

"Glory be!" said Miss Barrow. "Well, I can guarantee that it didn't happen while I was with them. And you know me, Kathryn. I'm—ubiquitous."

Even as she hung up, Miss Stone was planning her interview with Mrs. Rhodes, house mother of Dolores's dormitory. It was only nine-thirty, and Mrs. Rhodes would be on duty behind the desk in the foyer, checking her girls in from the library or from the other places on campus where they might have gone (for the girls were not permitted to leave campus except on week ends, and they signed in and out). The busiest hours for a house mother were from nine to eleven at night, and Mrs. Rhodes had some hours left to go until Lights Out, when she could gather the tatters of her private life around her and sit down to rest her feet. Mrs. Rhodes could not come to her. She would have to go to Mrs. Rhodes.

Not for the headmistress of Stone Oaks was the casual throwing on of a wrap and the impetuous dart out of doors. An example must be an example, always and interminably, or it is no example at all. She put on the beige wool coat lined with sheared beaver, the brown hat whose rim was bound in darker satin, her cream-colored doeskin gloves. Though she eyed her stadium boots rebelliously, she sat down dutifully and pulled them on. She walked into her bedroom to take a fresh white handkerchief from a drawer and paused to look at herself in the mirror as she unfolded it. "Very nice," said the mirror, "but aren't you making a tremendous fuss about nothing much? Why are you?" And, as clear as day, a small, flat voice in the back of her mind spoke up, "Because I don't like it, I distrust it, there is something wrong with it."

She had often argued with that small voice, because, like all cultivated women, she had come to be wary of instinct, of the devilish subconscious that could produce miraculously acceptable answers to hide its own dark designs. Perhaps this disturbance that she felt was nothing more than jealousy of a young and beautiful woman, or resentment of a passion that she herself had never known. Or perhaps she was just having a case of "nerves," that excuse that women of fifty employed to cover their accumulated inner anger. Whatever it was, she was definitely unhappy with it.

The wind had died down, but the snow had become more earnest. She walked along the gravel path beside the high stone wall that shut the school grounds off from suburban Philadelphia, past the tall iron gates with their inhospitable chain, up the walk to the wide white veranda of Alma House. From here she could see the lighted library clock and the study lamps glowing in the windows of the dormitory opposite. Five hundred girls lived in these enclosed acres. Five hundred lambs, not one of which must be allowed to turn black.

She entered the foyer and was greeted by the sight of Mrs. Rhodes coming down the carpeted stairs, her hands full of trembling pink blossoms.

"Beautiful?" said Mrs. Rhodes, raising the flowerpot. "Betsy Dermott gave it to me for helping her put a hem in a dinner dress. I adore cyclamen, don't you?"

Seemingly with no effort at all Mrs. Rhodes set the pot down on her desk, answered a belligerent phone, shoved a written message across to a waiting student, and beamed at Miss Stone. "I hope you've come to tell me that radios and record players are to be banned from the rooms, Miss Stone. It would be happy news for me."

"I'm sorry. The board hasn't been able to reach a decision. I've come to talk to you privately, if I may."

"Of course. Linda, dear, will you look after the desk for a few minutes? Miss Stone and I will be in my office."

Smiling and waving, responding to greetings in the manner of a popular prima donna, Mrs. Rhodes led the way down the hall to a small room inhabited by green filing cases. Only when the door was safely closed behind them did Mrs. Rhodes let her face relax into worry. "Is something wrong, Miss Stone?"

"I don't know, Mrs. Rhodes. Something has come up about Dolores Kennedy's week ends in New York, and I thought you could give me the information I need."

"Surely." Mrs. Rhodes sighed with relief. "I thought it would be something much worse than *that*. Dolores Kennedy is a darling child, and her uncle is a charming man. Charming."

"You've met him?"

"Oh no. But I've spoken with him on the telephone. Since Dolores was going to New York alone, I felt it my duty to call his residence and make sure that she had arrived safely."

Wonderful Mrs. Rhodes! "You called each time?"

"Oh yes. Mr. Canby made a joke about it. He said that we were getting to be fast telephone friends and that he was glad to see that his niece was in such devoted hands. Really, I think his reputation as a curmudgeon is quite unwarranted."

"I didn't know he had such a reputation."

Mrs. Rhodes looked as startled as if the headmistress had confessed an ignorance of the architectural merits of the Taj Mahal. "You know who he is. Winthrop Canby. Terribly rich old man, collects paintings, insults everyone he meets, writes wicked articles for the *Review* once in a while? You know."

"Of course," said Miss Stone slowly. "I remember now. There was a profile of him in *The New Yorker*. Man is nothing. Art is eternal. The only difference between women and vegetables is that vegetables are more interesting. I remember."

Mrs. Rhodes's soft pink face protested. "I think the newspapers have it in for him. I've found him most pleasant."

"You're sure it was Mr. Canby to whom you spoke?"

"Certainly. I've heard him on the radio. He's on Information, Please occasionally."

"I've always marveled," Miss Stone said, "that very intelligent men can have no morals at all. You'd think, since Mr. Canby is so smart, that he would have run his life a little better. His past is a shambles, and he makes no effort to hide it. Sometimes I've even suspected him of bragging about it. There's a limit to what the press can find out on its own."

"I put it all down to publicity. They crucify him because he's unusual, picturesque. But he's not nearly so bad as he's painted. I know."

Miss Stone told about the story Dolores had written, and Mrs. Rhodes giggled. "You mustn't pay any attention to a thing like that, Miss Stone. These girls are kept pretty close and they read a great deal. James Joyce and Hemingway and Maugham. You have to expect the biological urge to pop up somewhere, and on paper's a good safe place."

"We've considered that. I wish I'd brought the paper along. It's all about this girl and this man living together without benefit of clergy, and it seems astoundingly accurate to me."

Mrs. Rhodes patted her arm soothingly, her old-fashioned diamonds glittering from their high-pronged setting. "These children surprise me, too, once in a while. They give such an impression of sophistication, such an air of know-it-all, that I begin to worry. But, come to find out, it's only a disguise for their innocence. I ask a few blunt questions and all their pretense crumbles away. Sometimes they don't even understand the questions. Makes me feel like a dissolute old brothel-keeper instead of a respectable widow."

"Then you think we should let Dolores go again this week end?"

Mrs. Rhodes smoothed her glossy white pompadour thoughtfully. "Are you leaving the decision up to me?"

"I seem to be incapable of making it myself."

"I say she can't come to any harm with Mr. Canby. Since she's his sister's child, his past can't affect her. And Dolores is a remarkably well-behaved girl." She pursed her lips. "Besides, come to think of it Mr. Canby told me that he was leaving for Florida

23

the latter part of this month, so she won't have many more chances to visit."

Miss Stone rose promptly. "She will ask you our decision in the morning. Tell her that she may go."

"My stars, I hate to think that I've taken the responsibility for her all on my own shoulders. You've had more experience than I've had, and if you smell a rat—why, the rat might be there." Her soft face trembled like an abused baby's. "Miss Stone, I'd rather you made the decision."

The headmistress laughed and pulled on her gloves. "Let's compromise, then. She may go this time, but no more. How will that be?"

"Fine. Shall I tell her it's to be the last time?"

"Not until she comes back. No use giving her a deadline to be desperate about. You may send her to me if you like, and I'll tell her."

Mrs. Rhodes bustled happily to open the door. "Wonderful! I do hate disappointing my girls. Cowardly of me, but I can't seem to help it. And, really, I am very sure that Dolores is sound."

Well, there it was. All the evidence she had been able to gather had been in the girl's favor, and her intuitive alarm was silly and wrong. Still, back in her own sitting room, she sat down at the gilt desk and pulled out a sheet of notepaper. "Dear Mrs. Kennedy," she wrote. "I must ask your advice about your daughter's ——" No, that wasn't right. The Kennedys were paying a large sum of money to Miss Stone and the school, so that they need not worry about their daughter's behavior. They had hired Miss Stone to do a job, and it was only fair that she should do it without their being bothered. She crumpled the unfinished note in her hand and sighed. In spite of everything her faculty members had told her, she was certain that this was not the last of this little matter.

2

Dolores sat in her Pullman chair and smiled out at the flying landscape. Above the stark trees and grimy houses and snow-covered fields the sunset burned with an unbelievable ferocity. Letty, her mother's cook, had once kept such a sunset in her kitchen on a painted calendar, and Mr. Kennedy had winced whenever he looked at it.

"It's blinding, Letty."

"Sure is. That red and yaller, they're mighty fine colors."

"The man who painted that certainly improved on nature. I've never seen a sunset like it. Have you?"

"Lawd, Mr. Kennedy, sunset comes about dinnertime. I can't be foolin' around looking at no sunsets." She looked at the garish streaks of color proudly. "That's why I keep this picture by me, so I can see a sunset any old time."

"Well, if it does that much for you, Letty——"

She must remember to tell her father that he would be cured of his incredulity at the work of calendar designers if he would look out of the window at the right time on a certain kind of winter evening. And he must look very quickly. For in just these few minutes the flares in the west had dwindled, the shouting red had turned to tender mauve, the yellow to a gentle green. A rare and beautiful sky for a rare and beautiful occasion—the miracle of her being allowed to go to New York again.

The lights in the car went on and she looked at her watch.

Nearly six. At this hour Richard was leaving the university to catch his train, and in her uncle's apartment the Chinese boy was beginning to set the table for three. Time to go to freshen herself. Her hand reached to the place on the green plush beside her where her purse should be—and encountered nothing. The purse was not there. She bent to look underneath her chair, ran her hands around the lining of the seat cushion, shook the folds of her coat. The gray leather envelope had disappeared.

She glanced around the car, half-filled with dozing or reading strangers. Unlikely that anyone should have walked by while she was looking out the window, picked up her purse, and returned to his chair. If it had been stolen, the thief was in some other car by now, grieving over the poor haul he had made. But it was much more probable that there had been no thief, that she had dropped it somewhere in the train in the process of getting settled. Frowning, she tried to recall when she had seen it last.

But—again, the miracle—before she could think, the porter was holding the purse under her eyes. "This yours, miss?"

"Oh yes. Thank you very much. I'd just missed it."

"Lady back there picked it up off the floor a while ago. Said when she saw you begin to hunt, she knew it must be yours."

She half-turned in her chair, ready to smile her thanks at the good Samaritan. "Which lady?"

"The one in the little black hat with the veil over her nose. She's not looking this way right now." As he took his tip he said impassively, "Better check and make sure everything's all there. Lady looks good, but you never can tell."

Impossible to explain to him that she could not insult the finder by riffling through the purse in front of her. The Stone Oaks code was explicit: Better to be robbed than to risk giving offense to an innocent person. Swaying down the aisle on her way to the ladies' room, she paused beside the smart little black hat. "Thank you very much. I'm sorry to have been so careless."

As the wearer of the hat turned her head, Dolores saw that she was not so mature as she had seemed at a distance. In spite of her severe *tailleur*, she was no more than a year or two older than Dolores herself. "Perfectly all right," said the girl crisply, and turned her face again toward the black window. Dismissal, and a rather abrupt dismissal at that.

The ladies' room was empty, and Dolores sat down before a mirror, wondering. She could take an oath that she had never seen the curt young lady before in her life, and yet the face was disturbingly familiar. Who else had had that curve of cheek and straight line of nose, the black hair and the wide-spaced eyes? The answer came to her suddenly as she was putting away her powder puff and made her smile at her own reflection. The young lady looked like Dolores! Not terribly alike, but something like. It would take another look to tell the exact degree of similarity. But when she returned to her chair the other girl was no longer in the car, nor did she reappear.

The little incident left her mind completely in the excitement of leaving the train and finding a cab. A shiny new cab for a change, with an efficient and uncommunicative driver. She sat back and pictured Uncle Winthrop struggling from his bed, shouting his discomfort as his valet sought to encase his ailing body in dinner clothes, hobbling out to the dining room to open his decanters and make the cocktails himself. He was not an old man. Fiftyish. But his illness had increased his natural irascibility until even his pampered servants trembled when he spoke. A month ago, the first time she had come for cocktails and dinner, Dolores had trembled too.

Watching him churn the shaker fiercely, she had said, "It's very good of you to trouble with us."

"Trouble? My dear girl, I never do anything I don't want to do, and I recommend that principle as the only sane one around which to build a life. No, the fact is that I met your young man a couple of weeks ago and was much impressed." His black eyes held a satiric glitter. "Surely your mother doesn't approve of him. It was an unwritten law in our family that when I admired someone, everyone else should be revolted by him. Last young man in the world I should have expected you to choose."

"I've known him since we were children."

"A case of proximity, then. I should have realized that you were quite incapable of appreciating his finer points. Perhaps that's the

27

very reason you'll make a good wife for him." Chuckling, he handed her a glass. "I enjoy cocktails twice as much since my doctors have absolutely forbidden me to have them."

"Shouldn't we wait for Richard?"

"Not at all. He can't get here until seven-thirty, and the moment his foot crosses the threshold we go in to dinner. It takes two hours to consume my food properly, and I have an appointment later. Anyway, Richard doesn't need liquor. He has something better. Youth."

She laughed, sipping her drink. "So do I, Uncle Win."

"So you do, my pet. Also you have many grave inhibitions. Which Richard has not."

A far cry from that first timidity to the confident eagerness with which she hurried toward her uncle now. Flattering to have, even for an hour, the sole attention of a man who refused twenty invitations a day. Fascinating to listen to his monologues, vivid and racy talk which her mother would have said was unfit for a young woman's ears but which opened a new world to her, a wonderful wide world bounded, not by tiresome codes or by tedious conventions, but by simple inclination. Wonderful to be treated as an adult, she who was everywhere else treated as half-child. Fast as the cab was going, she wished it faster.

The taxi driver said over his shoulder, "You being followed, miss?"

"Followed?" She leaned forward, not sure that she had heard correctly.

"I didn't mean the cops was on your trail or nothin'. Just thought somebody else from the station might be going to the same place. Another taxi's been on our heels the whole time. It's got one headlight much dimmer than the other, that's how I know."

She twisted to look out the back window. "Perhaps my uncle went to the station to meet me and we missed each other somehow."

"I don't think he wants to catch up, but I'll slow down and give him a chance." He slowed the cab to a snail's pace, studying the rear-view mirror. "No dice. He's slowing too."

"It must be purely coincidental. I can't imagine why anyone would follow me." In the darkness she caught her lower lip between her teeth, to suppress her amusement at the ridiculous idea.

"You're a cute enough kid. Might be a masher. If it is, he don't give up easy. Mighty long drive out this way. I'll just put my monkey wrench on the seat beside me, in case he tries to get funny."

The businesslike way in which he located the heavy tool and prepared for violence impressed her. For five minutes she sat quietly in her corner, while he increased speed, slackened speed, passed other cars, or hung behind them. "Nope," he said finally. "Somebody just wants to see where you're going. Want to get a look at him?"

"But if he won't pass us——"

"There's tricks to all trades. I can make him pass us."

He accelerated abruptly, sped around a sudden corner, raced down a block, turned again, and drew up at the curb in front of an isolated drugstore. "Street light and neon sign," he said. "You ought to get a good look at him. Here they come."

Another cab roared around the corner, hesitated a second, slid on by, its taillights receding rapidly. Her driver snickered. "Well, they know we're on to 'em now. Anybody you recognize, lady?"

At last she was disturbed. Could coincidence be stretched this far? "All I could see was his overcoat and his hatbrim. It wasn't my uncle or my fiancé, though. I'm sure of that much."

The driver put his cab in gear and pulled smoothly away from the curb. "A heavy-shouldered gent in a light gray overcoat. Do you want I should tell the next cop we see? Might be a good idea."

They came to the tremendous apartment house without seeing a policeman, however, and she was glad. Melodrama was bad taste, and there is no situation more melodramatic than that of the pursuer and the pursued. The officer might write down their story soberly, but he would be thinking, "Dear God, deliver me from these fairy tales that come out of the heads of impressionable young things who let themselves be frightened by people who have seen too many movies." Smiling, he would turn in the report to his superior, and that would be the end of it. Unless a newspaper reporter happened to be standing near by and caught the name of the girl. "Dolores Kennedy? Goes to Stone Oaks? That's an expensive school. Where's she from? Holy Moses, those are the River Island Kennedys! Say, give me a little more of the dope on this, will you?" Far better to rest in the hope that the other cab had merely chanced to be going the same way, and say nothing.

The cabdriver, bereft of a suitable climax, accepted her thanks and her tip without relish. "I'll watch you in," he said, "and take my advice, lady, don't come out alone any more tonight. Just because we haven't seen 'em again doesn't mean they've given up. They mighta just got smarter."

And sure enough, after she had taken the elevator to the fourth floor, she looked out the window and saw him still standing there beside his cab, sturdy and alert, the entrance lights gleaming on his leather jacket. As she watched, he climbed into his cab and drove away, and with him went the little fears he had inspired. As she tapped on her uncle's door she was smiling again, dismissing the whole incident from her mind as one dismisses a ghost story when the chills have dissolved into plain improbability.

Then Ching opened the door, and she walked into the magic land of which she had dreamed every minute of the five days she had been away from it. Even the air was different here, and as she took off her coat and folded her gloves she savored it, pulling its faint fragrance into her lungs, exhaling slowly. Nothing had changed, all was still as it had been. The wide, gracious rooms spread before her as humbly as if she were their mistress and not a still-timid guest, and down that little hall was the bedroom where delight must still be shimmering in the intimate air. It was all as beautiful as a dream castle, and as evanescent; well she knew that a stamp of her mother's foot or a stroke of Miss Stone's pen could make it disappear.

In the living room the frosted shaker sat on its silver tray waiting, and the birch logs sizzled pleasantly in the fireplace. From the adjoining study she heard her uncle's voice talking into the telephone.

"Just came in this minute," he was saying. "Yes, she's right here. Not at all. If she hadn't been a bit tardy, I shouldn't have had the chance for a delightful conversation. Thank you, Mrs. Rhodes. I'll keep an avuncular eye on her."

He came bustling toward her, a little man whose fierceness belied his size. "At long last!" he said indignantly. "Do you realize that by dallying you have kept me talking to that female watchdog for five minutes? Am I to be spared nothing?"

"Mrs. Rhodes likes to talk to you," she said demurely. "She adores you."

"Of course she does. It's my fate to charm only those women whom I most despise." He said more kindly, "Sit down, my dear. I dislike having you tower over me. Tell me, what kept you?"

"The driver came a different way."

"And a longer one, I'll be bound." He handed her a small round glass and scowled at her upturned face. "Stop looking like your mother, Dolores. Stop it this minute!"

Obediently she dropped her eyes, but she was saddened. This was the one jarring note in their relationship, his hatred of her mother, and she felt like a traitor for not having the courage to make a stand against it. Her mother was everything that was lovely and kind, everything that Dolores should be and was not, and it was hard to be evasive or apologetic for her. "I suppose I do look a great deal like her," she said softly.

"Thank God the resemblance is only external. You have imagination and fire, and Celeste has always been placid clay." His voice grew gentler. "I am not an emotional man, and what emotions I have I manage to rationalize away. Except my feelings toward my sister, which began early and go too deep for rationalization. Jealousy is the most accurate name for them, I suppose. But how can one be jealous of everything one disapproves?"

"I don't know. She isn't jealous of you."

"If she were, I could like her better. Or if she were stubborn or belligerent. But no. I was five years her senior, and from the moment she was born she wiped me out. Yet I was the more intelligent, the more active, the more creative." He rubbed his arthritic knee with a grimace of discomfort. "But she was good, and the power of sheer goodness is that it minimizes every other virtue. Intelligence is nothing compared to it, and an adventurous spirit

31

is its enemy. The family talked about her wonderful disposition and her manners and her dependability, and I was cast into outer darkness. The worst of it was that, while my struggles and shoutings annoyed the family and made them angry, Celeste *forgave* me. Actually. Forgiveness—the great indifference, the supreme insolence—that's what I had of her, and our parents thought I should be happy with it!"

"It's only that she tries to overlook people's faults, Uncle Win."

"Exactly. And what impertinence, to decide that certain characteristics are faults and so ignore them! Especially when those faults might be considered virtues under more judicious eyes." He sat back and looked pleased. "I tried to kill her once, when I was fifteen and she was ten."

She laughed, recognizing the gambit of wild overstatement with which he always began one of his amusing fairy tales. "I take it the attempt wasn't successful."

He smiled, too, his infrequent, shy smile. "No. It was a very mild effort. She used to like to take walks along a path that skirted the edge of the cliff by the river. Does she still?"

"She and Dad walk there once in a while on Sunday afternoons. There's an iron railing all along the edge now."

"There wasn't then. Well, Mother and Dad didn't like to forbid her to go—they never forbade her anything—but it used to make them anxious. And I used to do everything I could to get her to walk there more often. I showed her pictures in my botany book and hinted that the best specimens in the world were found in high, inaccessible places. I told her stories of mountains she might climb someday, if she grew sure-footed enough. I even lent her my treasured binoculars, so that she would be distracted from watching her way, lean over too far perhaps. But all that ever happened was that I suffered agonies of suspense every time she set out and paroxysms of mortification every time she returned, as healthy and bouncing as when she had gone." He shook his head wryly. "Worst of all, she did find some rather rare wild flowers. There was a piece about them in the paper, and the family was terribly pleased."

"Compared to the physical violence most brothers inflict on their sisters, yours was no murder attempt at all."

32

"I told you it was mild. The amazing thing is that, young as I was, I had the right idea. The best murders shouldn't look like murder at all. They should—and do—look like accidents."

"Then how can you tell whether——"

"You can't, that's the beauty of it. But if you have a suspicious nature and an eye for motive—well, all these little stories in the daily papers about wives falling off of stepladders and husbands slipping in bathtubs and children who are left alone just long enough to get into some fatal mischief begin to make sense." He waved his glass at her. "Let's go at this logically. Whom do you want to kill?"

"Nobody," she said, startled.

"Naturally someone who is closely associated with you. Why? Because people you dislike who stay away from you cannot be annoying. It's the people you live with who get on your nerves. The police tell me—I've done some research, I'm writing a monograph on the subject—that nine murders out of ten are done within the confines of the family. Now it's obvious that suspicion, once aroused, will fall on the members of the victim's family, so the clever murderer sees to it that suspicion isn't aroused at all. He arranges an accident—a believable act of God—and, if he's smart enough, he makes the very habits and inclinations of his victim work for him. As I tried to do with my sister Celeste."

She said, with mock-seriousness, "Promise me one thing, Uncle Win. The minute I begin getting on your nerves, tell me."

Through his laughter she heard Ching open the front door, and her pulses began a light, rapid beat. Richard had arrived. As he took off his coat in the hall, she caught glimpses of his tall young back, saw him smooth his close-clipped curly hair and slap his pockets to make sure his cigarettes were there. He came in, walking his swift, imperious walk, and there was no flaw in him. Shaking hands with her small fiery uncle, he seemed a sunlit Apollo bending to a black, crippled Vulcan.

"You're early," said her uncle sourly.

Richard smiled. "Glad to see you, too, Mr. Canby."

Then he was bending to kiss her cheek, and now she could perceive the immoderate happiness in his face, the open possessiveness of his manner, and she was alarmed. Her uncle's eyes were sharp. He was a magpie for secrets or delicate situations, pouncing on their merest glitter, tucking them away in his memory until they could serve a public and dramatic moment. While Richard's head was on a level with her own, she shook her head ever so slightly in warning.

He knew at once what she meant. Taking a chair on the other side of the fireplace, he gave his whole attention to Uncle Win, who was grumbling that in all his life he had never known a train to be so early.

"I didn't take the train I usually do," Richard said. "I had to come up earlier for an appointment, and it didn't last as long as I had expected it to."

Uncle Win grudgingly handed him a glass. "Probably had a tea date with a female, and she turned you down, so you thought you'd run in here and upset all my arrangements."

Richard grinned. "I can see it won't do any good to tell you I was at the dentist's."

"With that aura of well-being shining out all over you? Even Dolores wouldn't believe it." He turned to his niece with relish. "Don't let him play Galahad for you. I caught him once, dining with a most attractive redheaded creature, and I had to stand there for a solid ten minutes before he summoned the grace to introduce me. Parks, her name was."

Richard winked at her. "All this because I got here a measly ten minutes early. I was a fool not to walk back and forth in the rain for another half-hour."

"When you came in," she said, "he was in the midst of explaining how he would go about killing someone."

"Murder? I would have said that torture was more his dish."

Uncle Win beamed. "I take that as a compliment to my subtle nature. The conclusion—which your entrance prevented me from stating—is that everyone has tried to kill somebody at one time or another."

"I haven't," said Richard thoughtfully. "I've come close to killing myself, though. Polo ponies and speedboats."

34

"My mother," said Dolores, "used to insist that you were trying to kill me. The tiger traps. Remember?"

"My God, yes. Now I do. One of them broke your leg, didn't it?"

She heard his voice telling the story to Uncle Win, and she leaned back and closed her eyes.

The first time she had heard of Richard she was eight years old and playing with her doll on the floor. Her mother and Mrs. Jordan —Aunt Alice, by courtesy and affection—were sitting in the wide living room of the Kennedy house on a summer afternoon, and the scent of the garden roses and the plashing of the bright river that encircled the island mingled with the soft flow of their voices and the discreet clink of their teacups.

"You don't think I'm too old to be a good mother to him, do you, Celeste? Frank is wild to take him, and we can afford it."

Her mother smiled at the little girl on the floor. "It's the best thing you could do. If another youngster doesn't come our way pretty soon, I'll be tempted to adopt one myself. We never wanted Dolores to be an only child, and she's already eight years old."

Aunt Alice lifted Dolores and her doll into her silken lap. "Darling, a little boy named Richard, ten years old, is coming to live at my house and be my little boy. When you come over to see me, you can play with him. Won't that be nice?"

The radiance on her face led Dolores to believe that the little boy would be Prince Charming himself. Yet when she first saw him her immaculate little soul disapproved. He was digging a large hole in the Jordan back yard, and he was dirt and sweat from head to foot; and, worse, with one defiant stare he made her feel as if he was doing an important work in the world and that she, in her fresh pinafore with her doll under her arm, was a silly and inferior person. Resentment curdled her good manners.

"What's that awful hole for?" she asked scornfully.

"Tiger trap." Though he was standing at the bottom of the hole, he seemed to be looking down at her, from the height of his immeasurable superiority. "It's going to have leaves and branches over

35

it when it's finished. I've got 'em all over the place, so you better be careful where you walk."

"Did Aunt Alice say you could dig them?"

He was mildly curious. "Is my—mother—your aunt?"

"Not really." She tossed her black curls importantly. "She's a Friend of the Family. I've known her all my life. I'm Dolores Kennedy."

Feigning a staggering wonderment, he said, "No kiddin'." Immediately he began to dig again, plainly dismissing any further conversation with her as a ridiculous waste of his time.

It was a new and wrenching experience for a little girl who was accustomed to nothing but love and praise, and she walked home angrily, vowing that she would never go back. But she did go back, again and again, finding haven with Aunt Alice when his lordly indifference became too much for her. She learned that he had been made to fill in the tiger traps, and she felt a little regret, because it had been an exciting idea. The well-fed, soberly tended River Island children she knew had never attempted anything so venturesome as tiger traps.

Naturally there was one he had forgotten. Taking her usual path through the hedge, weeks later, she stopped on the edge of the lawn behind a lilac bush to watch him playing ball with two other boys. The game was not going well, and the quiet was reft by complaints and angry accusations. Softly, lest she offer herself as a target for their accumulated anger, she made for the Jordan side porch—and fell crashingly into the leaf-covered pit.

Her leg did not hurt her at once. She lay there, helpless and stunned, but not uncomfortable. Dimly she saw Richard's awe-stricken face peering over the edge at her. "Goddlemighty!" he was shouting. "The thing works. It actually works!"

Then the enormity of his fault dawned on him and he reached out a hand to her. "Don't just lay there," he said anxiously. "You aren't hurt, are you?"

It was the first time he had paid her any real attention.

Her uncle was speaking to her. "He left that hole there on purpose, you know. Not consciously but, as Freud would say, he'd

36

forgotten it for a reason. Mrs. Jordan was the prize and the two of you were contending for her. He taught you that you were the intruder, not he. With a broken leg, you couldn't come over for a while. He put you out of the running very neatly."

Richard asked reasonably, "Does Freud say how I knew it would break her leg?"

"You didn't know. You could only pray." He struggled to his feet. "Dinner, children." He hurried ahead, leaving them momentarily to their own devices.

Richard took her arm. "How are you?" he asked softly. "I haven't had a chance to find out."

"I'm fine." She leaned against him for a second as they walked, openly loving, openly beloved, drenched in the new tenderness that had been born only the week before in the bedroom down the hall. She had been frightened by the emotion then, fought against it, resisted the intimacy toward which it impelled her, until Richard, perplexed and exhausted, had fallen asleep beside her; and, watching him, she had been filled with such a tremulous gentleness that she could hardly bear to wake him up and get him out of the house before her uncle's return. Tonight she would not send him away. "I love you," she said.

He squeezed her arm absent-mindedly, and his face was serious and brooding. "I wish your uncle didn't worry me. I wish I knew what his game is."

"Game?"

"Why he has us here at all, what the whole thing's about. God knows it's a present from heaven, but I don't get the idea."

The tender dream in which she had been lost dissolved and let her down into reality with a bump. She took her seat at the elaborate table unhappily. How serene life had been when she was allowed to believe that everyone meant what he said and did thoughtful things for the pleasure of doing them! Time to get over that, time to take on the hateful disadvantages of being an adult— the suspicion, the questioning of motives, the weighing of chances. There must be a reason for her uncle's sudden interest in her, of course, and, if Richard thought so, it was important to discover what that reason was. She ate her chilled fruit and watched the faint movement of the white orchids in the centerpiece and thought.

Champagne with the dinner, and brandy and coffee in the living room afterward. Liquor had a strange effect on her. On other people it bestowed confidence and well-being; to her it brought uncertainty and self-disapproval. Its fumes warmed the doubt already in her heart, and the doubt expanded, breaking the golden mood of the evening, revealing the bleak clay shards of which beauty had been made. What she had called love was wantonness; her uncle's interest was a mask for a dark ulterior; enchantment had been rooted in shallow flattery and muddy beguilement. She pushed the brandy glass away, picked up her coffee cup, tried to smile at Uncle Win as he prepared to take his departure. (A black cape on a man was not romantic, it was ridiculous.)

He looked at the two of them with a wry benevolence. "I shall be home at two o'clock. If you go out, be sure that Ching gives you a key before he leaves." (His smirk belied the idea that they would go anywhere but into each other's arms. How shabby that it should be true!) "I hope, however, that you'll stay in and discuss a little proposition I have put to you." From among the black folds he pulled out a large white envelope and tossed it to Richard. "I've had it put in legal style to show you that I'm very much in earnest. Good night." The door closed solidly behind him.

Richard laughed. His misgivings had vanished with the wine. "He's a dramatic little guy, isn't he?" he said. He threw the envelope on the coffee table, pulled her out of her chair, kissed her, held her close. For an interval there was no sound but the grasping of the fire and his quick breath storming in her inner ear. "After Ching leaves, darling. As soon as he leaves——"

"No." The word came without her volition, flat and hard.

He dropped his arms as if she had struck him. "You promised that this time—— You promised."

Instinct prompted her, chillingly. "I can't. Not here."

"That's a pretext," he said slowly. "This is the only place where we can be private. If not here, then nowhere."

Wretchedly she sought for words that would explain her revul-

38

sion. This was a contrived situation, of her uncle's making, and she rebelled at acting her part like a puppet on a string. Whatever she did now would not be spontaneous, and hence not delightful. But how could she explain this to Richard without seeming foolishly obstinate or oversensitive? "I can't help it," she said. "I'm sorry."

"I see."

But he didn't see. Under his cool civility was the hot humiliation of her refusal, and she was distressed. "Richard——" she began, pleadingly.

He would not have her consolation. He engrossed himself in tearing open the white envelope. "Might as well find out what your uncle has on his mind," he said.

While he read, she busied herself with little acts of repentance, filling his coffee cup, pushing an ash tray nearer. She would have liked to stroke his hair or take his hand, but he was proud and, having offended him, she did not dare. Instead, she sat opposite him and waited until he raised a stunned face and noticed her.

"He'll give us two hundred thousand dollars if we get married before he leaves for Florida. That's in two weeks." Wonderingly, he handed the papers across to her. "He's out of his mind. Read it."

She picked up the note that her uncle had clipped to the document.

I am fond of the two of you, and I dislike seeing you misled by fancy and empty promises. I know those promises. I believed them once myself.

From bits of information which come to me from here and there, I know that the Kennedys, at least, have no intention of allowing your marriage to take place. They won't come right out and say so. They'll go about the matter indirectly. First, it will be that Richard needs time to get started on his law career ("he should certainly be earning as much as your father is willing to give you for an allowance. You're both young. If he loves you, he'll be faithful"); next, they'll need Dolores at home for a while ("your mother's health has been failing, a trip might do her good but I

·can't get away from the office and I don't want her to go alone");
and then there'll be some other delay, until finally the marriage
will be waited out of existence. The truth, which they'll never tell
you, is that Richard isn't their kind. They want a sober, settled,
responsible Moneyman, who'll come eat their Sunday dinners,
bring up his children in the Episcopalian fold, and nod his head at
the windy wisdom of his elders. Richard, you see, is young and
charming enough to win you right away from them, and they're
not prepared to stand for that.

With money, you won't have to wait on their permission. The
Jordans haven't a great deal these days, and the Kennedys will sit
on theirs if you defy them. So, enter the romantic old uncle. This
contract says that, if your marriage takes place within the next two
weeks, a sum of two hundred thousand dollars will revert to you,
jointly. You need not thank me for this offer. Call it a whim, but
say that I can afford it.

Tears of self-reproach came to her eyes. "I've been misjudging
him. He's very kind."

"No one is ever kind two hundred thousand dollars' worth.
There's something else behind it." He took the papers, threw them
back on the table. "Whatever it is, he's finished my chances. If I
marry you now, I'm a fortune hunter for sure. If I try to marry you
later, I may not get you. I can't win." He looked down at her
somberly. "Honest to God, Dolores, it was never your money I
thought of. If you didn't have a dime, I wouldn't care. You were
always the top limb of the tree, the farthest star, the seventh wonder of the world, to me. As long as you know that, as long as you'll
have me, let's not fret about money or time or anything else. It
won't be as bad as your uncle says."

She smiled, but she was troubled. There were things that she
knew and he did not. Her family's sanction had been halfhearted.
Aunt Alice and her mother were not the friends they once had
been, and the hidden break between them might well be rooted in
this proposed match. The last year or two, either the Jordans or the
Kennedys had traveled south or west or east for as much of the
school holiday as they could; and, though she had accepted the

40

separation from Richard without question, it seemed to her now that such consistency was ominous. "He could be right," she said slowly.

"He doesn't look at things straight. You know. He always gets them crooked. I won't go so far as to say he's insane, but his mind's warped. It's what makes him different, it's why we like him, but it's dangerous to go by what he says, all the same."

She was not listening. Her mind ranged the past, picking up a phrase here, a gesture there, arranging them in a significant pattern, and she could see that, by smiling deception, her parents had led her to the very brink of betrayal and tragedy. There was no time for mourning. Stubbornly she began ticking off a list on her fingers. "Tomorrow we'll have the blood tests. Sunday we ought to look for a little apartment—for week ends. Even if Uncle Win offers us this place, I wouldn't want it. Not any more. Just a couple of rooms for our very own, where nobody can come in unless we say they may."

He stared at her as if she were speaking Greek. "You mean you want to get married next week end? But your parents. You've forgotten——"

An ugly little pang cut her heart, but her smile was unwavering. "I've never crossed them in my life before, but they haven't played fair. I love them, but they're wrong about this."

"You're taking your uncle's word for that. They may not feel the way he says they do." He took both her hands. "I'm not trying to talk you out of this, Dolores. I feel like standing up and cheering. But I know how you feel about your people, and I don't want you to have any regrets afterward."

Learning to think for oneself was like learning to walk: every step became more certain than the one before it. "We won't tell them. We'll keep it a secret. Then, if they're being honest with us, we can be married all over again next August with no one the wiser. And—if they were lying—why, we'll be married already and there won't be anything they can do about it."

She buried her head in his shoulder. It was not seemly that a bride should weep at the setting of her wedding day.

3

She returned to Stone Oaks in the early Sunday-evening twilight, just as Mr. Granahan, the night watchman, was taking his place in the little stone cubbyhole by the gate. He was a ruddy, good-natured man with a body that was shaped like a turnip, the big shoulders and deep chest dwindling to thin hips and lean shanks, and, so deep was his respect for Miss Stone, that not a girl had ever been known to bribe her way in or out after hours. She smiled at him as she pushed the gate open, and he leaned out of his little window to see her better.

"Well, Miss Kennedy. Have a nice trip?"

"Very nice. The weather's been so fine."

He drew experimentally on his pipe. "Depends on how you look at it. When you have to walk the grounds all night, no weather's fine enough except in summer. Don't happen to have a can of pipe tobacco on you, do you?"

She set her suitcase down on the walk. "I'll run down to the corner and get you some if you need it, Mr. Granahan."

"Good gosh, no! I was only kidding." But the offer had pleased him. He stepped out of his booth companionably. "Come to think of it, there *is* something you can do for me. I'd like the word to get around school that the place down on the north wall where somebody's been climbing in and out behind my back has been fixed. If you'll just mention—like you'd noticed it yourself—that there's a batch of barbed wire strung along the top there now, it'll save some young lady a heap of trouble."

"I'll mention it, but I can't promise that the right girl will hear of it."

He picked up the suitcase and handed it to her. "Oh, they'll hear about it all right. What one person knows around here, everybody knows."

That was true. Walking up to Alma House in the dimness under the gaunt, creaking elms, she heard the laughter of the girls coming out of the dining hall and felt a weakness in her knees. The blood tests, the procuring of the license, the finding of the little apartment, that had been the easy part; the difficult thing was going to be the keeping of the secret, not only for this week which preceded her marriage, but afterward as well. With all the bright, curious eyes fixed on her, she would never be certain of what they were seeing, of how much betrayal lay in a gesture or a mood. One whisper of rumor would start them belling on the trail to certainty, and she would be lost. Stone Oaks tolerated no married students, and expulsion would drive her back to River Island or to an open break with her parents. Tremulously, her nerves shrieking for courage, she stepped inside the foyer of Alma House.

To her relief, the front desk was deserted. Only Laura Derby, the Boston girl who roomed across the hall from her, was there, sorting her mail by the counter. Of all the girls in school, she liked Laura best. There was something direct and friendly and safe about Laura.

"Home from the big city," said Laura. "I hope you've had your dinner. They served half an hour early tonight because of the music program for vespers. You going to it?"

"I can't. I'll have to study."

"That's why I never take week ends off. I hate to pay the piper when I get back." She hooked arms with Dolores and walked with her up the stairs. "You're taking an English major, aren't you? Lucky you. When I had only psychology to contend with, I could go and eat meals just like other people. Since I added philosophy, I've been living on sandwiches in my room. The reason you've never heard of a fat philosopher is that they don't have time for food. I spent today composing a gemlike thesis on 'The Hedonism of Aristippus and Epicurus.' It's a lovely thing. I can't understand a word of it." They paused in the hall between their two doorways. "I have some coffee that's still hot. Want to come in and have a cup?"

"If you'll make me leave in ten minutes. I have to do a paper on the Romantic poets tonight, and I ought to get at it while everything's so beautifully quiet."

She threw her suitcase and her coat and hat on the coral-covered day bed in her room, put a fresh pack of cigarettes from a bureau drawer into her purse, and went back to Laura. In Laura's big wing chair, with a cup of coffee at her elbow and the faint melody of the vesper bell outside in the wintry dusk, her tight nerves uncurled, leaving her limp and peaceful for the first time in weeks.

"I wish we'd done this long ago," she said shyly.

"So do I. I've thought of it a good many times, but we're both the kind who keep to ourselves rather. And here we are, seniors, with only till June to go, so it's now or never." She glanced toward the open door and lowered her voice. "I think there's something you ought to know. I had to chase Annabelle Adams out of your room Saturday evening."

"What on earth was she doing there?" Stone Oaks doors might be closed, but they were never locked. It was an unwritten law that no one should enter a room without its owner's permission.

"When I saw her, she was sitting in a chair, waiting for you, she said. Of course she knew perfectly well that you were away, there's not a thing goes on around here that the creature doesn't know. I was polite but firm, and she put on that funny, vague look of hers and mumbled something about having an appointment with you. Did she?"

"No. I've spent half my life dodging Annabelle. She comes from River Island, too, but we weren't friends there, either." How short-lived the peaceful feeling had been. Even though her room was blameless—she threw away letters as soon as she had answered them, there was no space for keeping them—it was a worry to have malice prowling there. "What did she do then?"

"Fastened on me like a leech, had the nerve to follow me in here,

44

though she could see I was working my head off." Laura leaned back complacently. "It took me twenty minutes to get rid of her, but the time wasn't an absolute waste. I'm sure she'll never speak to me again."

"I wish I knew how to make her stop speaking to *me*," said Dolores wistfully.

"You're too polite, you'll never manage it. The girl's a psychopathic case. Rudeness isn't enough for her. It takes downright insult, and I don't think you're capable of it."

"She doesn't bother me often. I think she's lonely. She always wants to know what I've heard from home, and sometimes I feel sorry for her because she's so ugly."

"Don't let those scrawny legs and those buck teeth prejudice you in her favor," said Laura briskly. "She has a sly, mean little soul. Wanted to know if I'd heard about the ripe composition that dear Dolores had turned in to Miss Woods, full of the most intimate details, had the whole faculty on its ear. Annabelle was shocked but not surprised. Still waters run deep, she always says." She threw back her head and laughed.

Dolores set her cup down carefully. "How did she know anything about that?"

"I'm convinced that she listens at keyholes and her imagination does the rest." The laughter stopped suddenly. "I've worried you, and I thought you'd be amused. Please don't look like that. Nobody pays any attention to what Annabelle says, and I didn't think you would, either."

Her face was full of honest concern, and Dolores tried to smile. "The paper wasn't quite that bad."

"You don't have to tell me that. Anybody who knows you, even slightly, would know better."

"Still, since the idea is being spread around, I'd like to have a witness on my side." She reached for her purse. "Will you read it, Laura? It's the original and it's pretty badly scribbled, but you can make out what——" Her voice died while her hands rifled the purse, shook it, almost turned it inside out. When she spoke, her voice was faint and wavering. "I don't seem to have it with me. I thought I did."

45

"Could Annabelle have——"

"No. I had it with me when I started to New York. I—I must have lost it somewhere."

"It's probably blowing around the gutters of New York this very minute. Every time I open my bag to pay a taxi, I lose my driver's license and three sales slips."

Deep inside the purse her hand clutched the key to the door of the apartment she and Richard had found. It lay sweetly between her fingers, a talisman of happiness, lending to her some of the stanchness of its own metal. She found that she could smile at Laura's impersonation of Mrs. Rhodes's reaction to Clara Baugh's new French evening frock. "Honestly, Clara looked like the Arctic wastelands. Those vast, unbroken expanses of snow!"

Dolores giggled. The lost English paper suddenly seemed unimportant, and the little dark anxieties fled away.

Every morning, when the library chimes tolled seven, she got out of bed and ran to change the day on her little desk calendar. Monday gone, and Tuesday. She laughed at her excited face in the mirror, hummed a tune, and waltzed around the room while she dressed. But once outside her door, she turned sedate and usual, arranging her thoughts around Byron and Shelley and the mysteries of the Shakespearean sonnet. In class, she took down the next week's assignments carefully in her notebook, but next week was a myth in which she could not believe. Her imagination stopped at Saturday morning, when Time would drop over a cliff and splinter into brightness.

There were two letters waiting for her Wednesday afternoon when she came back from her classes, one from her father, one from Richard, lying side by side in friendly fashion in her mailbox. She read Richard's first, memorizing the time and place of their meeting, smiling at the vision of Uncle Win's sacrifice in getting up by nine o'clock to be a witness. "He wanted to take us somewhere to breakfast afterward, but I declined firmly on the grounds that we'd have little enough time to be by ourselves as it was. He protested that this was highhanded of me, considering that he was the genie in the bottle, but he finally gave in. If he hadn't been so involved in getting ready to leave for Florida—he goes the following week—

46

and trying to finish his essay on Murder, I think he'd have put up more of a fight. I love you, angel, but you do have some difficult relatives." This she destroyed, tearing it into such minute bits that even Annabelle Adams could never reassemble them.

Letters from her father were a rarity and she opened this one gently, apologizing to it for its having come off second best. As she read the words, she could hear her father's calm, pleasant voice saying them.

My dear:
  Things are very much as usual here, and we congratulate ourselves every day on having such an easy winter so far. In other parts of the country I suppose that, with two weeks still to go before Thanksgiving, winter hasn't even been mentioned yet. But you know how it snows and blows up here. No wonder we are winter-minded.

Thank God this is the last Thanksgiving you will have to be away from us. If I had it to do over again, I'd move nearer to Philadelphia, so that you could make it home for a day or two without going on safari. As one gets older, business affairs seem fairly unimportant in comparison to family ties. But, as your mother says, you will be home for keeps pretty soon. Will you have to spend Thanksgiving rattling around in a half-empty school? Or are you going home with one of the girls who lives nearer?

The Jordans are going to New Orleans for the Christmas vacation and, I guess, taking Richard with them. He has probably told you already, and the two of you have mourned together. I am sorry for you and glad for us. You must not begrudge our pleasure at the prospect of having you to ourselves for another little while before your Lochinvar carries you off for good.

And I shall be doubly glad to see you, because your mother's health has become a matter of great concern to me. She needs cheering up, and the sight of you will accomplish that.
          All our love,
            Dad

She covered her eyes with her hands and wept: first, that there should be so great a devotion in the lines; and second, that her father's love should be employed, as Uncle Win had said it would be, in an attempt to defraud her of the only thing she wanted.

By Thursday evening her excitement was so great that she could not settle down to anything. She crossed the hall and looked in on Laura, who was standing in a sea of white tissue paper and elegant boxes.

"Step over things and sit down," said Laura. "These lovely creations are my going-home trousseau. My mother likes to think that I keep myself stylish the year round, and I'm trying to keep up her illusions. At home, I do not wear the same green jersey dress day in and day out, so I always have to go out and buy a lot of stuff just before the holidays. There'd be no explaining to Mother that ordinarily I can't afford the time to be soignée."

Dolores picked up a wisp of green chiffon. "Oh, Laura! How could you bear to wear anything so beautiful to bed!"

"I couldn't, but I saw it in the showcase and something came over me. The saleslady simpered and asked, 'Does Moddom wish to take the nightdress with her?' And Moddom, trying to be airy, said, 'No. Just send it along.' I've been eating my heart out for it to get here ever since, and now it's too small."

"How awful." She held the nightgown to her shoulders, watched how the narrow pleats fell to the floor.

"I'm trying to take the disappointment as a judgment on me. 'Love not the world, nor the things that are in the world.' Serves me right. The way I felt about that nightgown was practically idol worship."

"Would you sell it to me, Laura? I'm sure it would fit me."

Laura's bright, dark eyes fastened on her with amusement. " 'Does Moddom wish to take it with her?' Sure, you can have it, but, I warn you, the price is astronomical."

"I don't care. It's worth it."

She noticed, while she was paying Laura, that her November allowance was nearly gone. There was only enough left to get her to New York and back once more, but that was all she needed. Surely she was entitled to one extravagant bit of adornment for her wedding day.

"I've been meaning to ask you," said Laura, "if you'd care to come home with me for Thanksgiving. I wrote to Mother and she says she'd love to have you."

She had not prepared herself for such a question. It took her too far into the uncharted future, involved a conflict between the subterranean part of her life and the obvious part. Her mind fumbled among possibilities.

"I don't know," she stammered. "I'd half-promised to——"

"Well, think it over. If you don't go to your uncle, come to us. It isn't so far from Eastern, and your fiancé might be able to make it down for an evening or two. We'd have fun."

"Thank you. I'd love to come, if I can arrange it."

She'd handled it badly. At best Laura must think her psychopathically timid; at worst, ungracious. Back in her room she found that her palms were wet from the little ordeal, and she laid the nightgown carefully down on her bed and wiped her hands with a towel. Outside her closed door she could hear the bustle of the girls going back and forth, the last strains of music from a radio before it would be shut off for study hours, the distant ringing of a telephone. She lay down on the bed, carefully avoiding the precious gown, and closed her eyes. If only excitement did not make her ill, now that there were so few hours to go!

A tap on the door brought her to a sitting position, but Annabelle was in the room before she could get to her feet, sliding toward the bed with a beribboned candy box under her arm, her light gray eyes avoiding Dolores's face.

"What a heavenly nightgown!" said Annabelle. "I don't blame you for just sitting down and admiring it. Why, it's positively— bridal!" She reached a hand toward it and Dolores gathered the gown up rudely, any old way, and shoved it inside a drawer. "Dolores, dear, I'm so sorry. Didn't you want me to see it? With it right in plain sight like that I didn't think——"

"Laura tells me that you were in here Saturday night," said Dolores stiffly.

"Yes. I thought I might borrow your notes on Byron, you told me once that I could. Heavens, the way Laura acted, you'd have thought I was a burglar. I had no idea that she'd constituted herself watchdog for this floor." She stood at the foot of the bed, slipping the purple ribbon from the chocolate box. "Have one?"

"No, thank you. I just finished dinner."

"They're from Garretson's. Make you feel as if you were back home again." She giggled. "Of course you may not *want* to feel that way. I wouldn't know."

Since taking a chocolate had somehow become an issue involving the affection she felt for her parents, she took one and ate it quickly. "It's very good," she said. But she would not ask Annabelle to sit down, chocolate or no chocolate. The two of them remained standing.

"How is Uncle Winthrop?" said Annabelle.

"Much better."

"How nice. The way Mrs. Rhodes spoke, she'd gotten the impression that he was at death's door. Queer how these things get twisted around, isn't it?" She smiled unpleasantly at a point a foot away from Dolores's head. "And Richard is as usual, I suppose?"

"Yes."

"I wrote Mother that I hadn't seen him in simply ages because you were spending your week ends in New York, and she seemed to be a little surprised at such—well, 'romantic goings-on,' she called them. But, my goodness, it isn't as if you had to climb the walls to get to see him. I told her that as long as the school gave you permission and you could go right in and out the front gate, why, nobody could possibly object."

There was no help for it, she was being driven to hatefulness. "About climbing walls," said Dolores. "Mr. Granahan says that somebody's been getting in and out over the north end somewhere. He's had to put barbed wire along the top."

"Surely you don't think that I——" She laid a virtuous hand on her narrow bosom.

"No. I told you because he wants the word to get around, and you're good at that sort of thing."

There was a silence, while Annabelle smiled and smiled and Dolores trembled at her own daring. Never before had she summoned the boldness to let Annabelle know, even indirectly, what she thought of her; and this was a poor time to have done it.

50

She hurried toward her desk. "If you still want those Byron notes, Annabelle, you're welcome to them."

"No, I don't need them now."

"Mine are pretty complete. There may be something in them you could use." She hated herself for the pleading note in her own voice, for her frantic little scramble to make amends, for the sheaf of papers she held out as an offering against retribution.

"No, thank you." Full of righteousness and outraged humility, Annabelle moved toward the door. But she had her moment of triumph. "Miss Stone would like to see you in her office right away," she said, and went out.

She sat in the narrow telephone booth and watched her tears drip down on the black mouthpiece and the pile of coins she had ready to appease the operator.

"Don't cry at me over the telephone," said Uncle Win irritably. "I can't make out what you're saying."

"Miss Stone won't let me come, Uncle Win. I'm not to leave the grounds until I go home for the Christmas holidays."

"I wouldn't pay any attention to that."

"I have to. They'll expel me if I don't."

"Don't be such a schoolgirl! What if they *do* expel you?"

"I couldn't let that happen," she said. "My family——"

She could not make him understand. He saw only that he was not to have his way, and he grew haughty and mean. "Unmitigated bosh!" he said. "What it boils down to is that two hundred thousand dollars isn't enough to suit you. You want to make sure of your father's money too."

"No, no——" She pressed a hand over her mouth to silence the noise of her weeping.

"What a sly little customer! I don't believe you meant to marry him at all. You could have done it last Sunday, if you'd wanted to. Oh, I know, there were the preliminaries to be gone through. But I have enough influence to hurry things like that along, and I wasn't asked. No, I very carefully was not asked."

"Please, Uncle Win. We didn't think——"

"And now you expect me to pull a magic rabbit out of a hat for

51

you. Well, I'm no longer in the mood. By next Wednesday my offer will have expired, and it will not be renewed. I'm afraid that you're really very much like your mother after all. My congratulations to you on the long and very dull life you're going to lead."

She had enough strength left to send a wire to Richard. Then she crept upstairs to her room and lay down on the bed to stare at the dark like a stone Niobe whose tears would never dry.

She had been ill, but she was better now. Vaguely she could recall walking over to the infirmary, supported by Laura and Mrs. Rhodes. And after that there were sporadic visions of Dr. Leonard plunging a needle into her arm, and of Nurse McCloskey holding a white basin while Dolores vomited. It was a whole week later before she could be cranked to a sitting position in the infirmary hospital bed and told that the diagnosis was a bad attack of tonsillitis with complications.

The throat had responded to penicillin, but Dr. Leonard was not through with the other aspects of the case. He was a quiet, urbane man with a large Philadelphia practice, and he was supposed to be at Stone Oaks only one day a week. Actually he came and went at all hours, being a victim of the notion that there were no such things as patients, but merely people who needed him. As he sat by the bed, taking her pulse, her eyes, weighed down with some soporific, took comfort in his beautiful tweeds, the whiteness of the cuff that slid back to reveal the dark springing hairs that began above his wrist, the firm fingers with a narrow white arch of nail at the tips.

"Better today," he said cheerfully.

"Yes. Much better."

"Throat sore at all?"

"No. A little swollen still, I think."

"That will go down in a day or so." He leaned back and smiled at her. "Well, you've given us quite a week of it, young lady."

The dreaminess persisted; she could not focus her attention sharply on anything. "I'm sorry," she said.

"There's nothing to apologize for. We don't think you succumbed to a strep germ on purpose." He looked down at the chart in his lap. "What did you have to eat last Thursday? Can you tell me?"

"Last Thursday? No, I don't remember."

"You ate all your meals in the school dining room?"

"Yes."

"Have anything between meals that came from outside?"

"No. I don't think I ate much that day."

"Something to drink, then? A cocktail somewhere?"

She wished he would go away, it was so much effort to answer. "No. I might have had a cup of coffee in Laura's room after lunch. We had coffee together several times last week."

"But you're not sure you had any that day?"

"It—seems to me we did. You could ask Laura. If it matters."

"You were extremely nauseated for two days. I'm trying to find out if you were poisoned." She turned her head wonderingly, and he laughed. "Food poisoning. Not arsenic."

"I ate a piece of candy that evening. Just one, out of a box that Annabelle Adams had."

"As an amateur psychologist, I am interested in why, when I said the word 'poison,' you responded with 'Annabelle Adams.' She's a girl you dislike?"

"Yes."

He was gratified at that, but he seemed to regard the candy as unimportant. "I'm inclined to believe, then, that the nausea was psychosomatic."

"I don't know what that means."

"It means that, the mind and body being of one piece, a struggle that goes on in one of them affects the other. You've been unhappy, had a sudden shock perhaps?"

"Yes. I've—had a shock."

He waited a moment, but she said no more, and he rose. "I've been keeping you under light sedation. Now that you're better we'll stop that, and the job of curing yourself will be up to you. The danger is that your emotional struggle will return, and you'll be too weak to cope with it. Try to ignore it, find something else to think about. Brooding will make you worse, might push you into some sort of silly behavior that you wouldn't attempt when you were well." He shook his head. "You're too young to be in such an abominable nervous state. What you need is courage, the self-generated variety, not the sort that comes from a needle."

All that afternoon she lay and looked at the white roses in a vase on the table, but not until evening did she manage to make the association between the flowers and a giver. Nurse McCloskey, coming in to remove the supper tray, was delighted to be asked.

"Shows you're beginning to sit up and take notice," she said. "They're from Richard Jordan. He was down here all last Saturday and Sunday trying to see you, but of course you were too sick to be seen. Throwing up, and a little out of your head with temperature. So he left the roses and went away."

Her mind was clearing. The sleepy wisps trailed away, leaving her worries and anxieties standing as stanchly as a city skyline when a fog lifts. "Was there a message with them?"

The nurse handed her a white sealed envelope and she held it in her hand while she was being made comfortable for the night.

"I won't look in again unless you ring," said Mrs. McCloskey. "There are two girls with measles in the contagion room, and what with the itching they don't sleep at all. I've used a gallon of calomine on them already. Have a good night, now."

In the solitude she rushed to read the note, tearing it open with gladness and anticipation.

> My darling;
> Don't worry about anything. Just get well. The plan had its drawbacks, as we both know, and it may be all for the best that things happened as they did.
> I am using the new address as a study hall for the little while left on it. The telephone number is Murray Hill 5-5420. If you cannot reach me at the school, the other number will find me. As soon as you let me know you are well enough, I'll come down to see you.
> Love,
> Richard

Incredulously she read it again. Then she snapped off the bed lamp and turned her face toward the wall, aching with rebuff, unable to bear the bright relief with which Richard had borne what to her was catastrophe. By morning she had conceived a plan based on two things: the fact that Mrs. McCloskey had not looked in on her once, and the realization that her room was on the first floor with only a low window sill and a hinged storm window between herself and where she wanted to be.

Friday morning she was permitted to sit up in a chair, and, when the nurse was out, she practiced walking on the sly. Weak, but not unsteady. Good enough for her purposes.

Taking her bedtime temperature, Nurse McCloskey raised her eyebrows. "A little too much exertion today, Miss Kennedy."

"I'm going to sleep this minute. What time is it?"

"Only seven-thirty. But a nice long sleep would be the best thing you could do for yourself. I'll see that you aren't bothered by messages or phone calls or the general Friday-evening rush."

She waited for half an hour before she rose and dressed in the dark. Everything was so wonderfully clear to her now, so beautifully simple. The important thing was to get herself safely married, make the wedding a *fait accompli*, before any machinations could upset her further. The money Uncle Win had withdrawn was not important, had never been important. Better this way, with no one in on the secret. Even if it were midnight by the time she reached Richard and the apartment, there would be someone, somewhere, who would perform the ceremony at that hour. Then Richard could come back with her on the three-thirty train, take a room in Philadelphia, and come to visit her in the infirmary on Saturday, just as if nothing had happened. Really, her illness had been a piece of good fortune, removing her from myriad-eyed Alma House.

Getting out of the grounds was easy. She stayed away from the walks, shielded herself with the shrubbery, waited for a moment when the gate was deserted, and slipped out, running from the yellow stain of the street light into the comfortable shadows. Her money was insufficient for indiscriminate taxi fares—she must keep some in reserve for an emergency en route—but the bus came promptly. Unfortunately its progress through the slushy streets was slow and she arrived at the station with not a minute to spare for a telephone call, but the little glow of self-admiration that she felt for her own venturesomeness triumphed over all obstacles. Richard would be there, anything else was inconceivable.

But by the time she reached New York and climbed the squeaking steps to stand in the dingy hallway outside the door of 4A, the glow was gone. The cold, the slush, the long train ride and the subway, the frigidity of her hands and feet and the ominous, dry heat of her forehead, these had killed it. She leaned against the doorjamb as she knocked, her ears confused with their own drumming and the noise of the traffic from the busy streets outside. A man ran down the staircase only ten feet away from her, and she did not even hear him until he had gone by. Not Richard, though. A big-shouldered man in a light gray overcoat and a hat pulled well down. She fitted her key into the lock and entered, leaning back against the door to close it.

He was not there. She knew it at once, for the one big room and adjoining bath was all that made up the apartment. The lamp by the desk had been left on, one of the day beds was rumpled as if he had napped there, his suitcase sat unopened by the wall. With his absence her lovely scheme evaporated, but she was not capable any longer of either tears or anger. Instead, and on her feet, she drifted toward exhausted slumber and jerked herself upright only in time. It was then that she saw, on the little hall table, the schedule of trains that ran between New York and Philadelphia, with a pencil mark encircling the nine o'clock westbound. They had passed each other in transit. The comedy of errors was complete.

At three in the morning, on a bad November night, the streets of Philadelphia were almost empty, but her hurrying footsteps on the pavement had a peculiar echo. Several times she looked back over her shoulder and, alarmed, saw nothing alarming. A few men, their shoulders presented diagonally to the wind, going their various ways to shelter. A policeman flashing his light into shop doorways. Still, when a stray cab came by, she was glad to hail it, thankful that she had the bare price of getting off the echoing streets. In the warmth of the heater she dozed off at once and was wakened by the voice of the cabdriver.

"This the corner you wanted, lady?"

"Yes." The listlessness of fever made her slow in finding the money for him.

Giving her the change, he said suspiciously, "The Stone Oaks entrance is half a mile on down. There ain't nothing here but a wall."

"I know. I'll be all right."

But within fifty paces she was not so sure. The echo behind her had returned, stopping when she stopped, beginning again when she began. Terror shook her. Two street lights lay between her and the light outside the main gate, bright havens of refuge in which she dared not show herself. She slipped into the tall bushes that fringed the wall and held her breath and listened.

There was no longer an echo on the walk. The intruder, too, must have taken to the softer ground. She could be sure of nothing, because the bushes around her sighed and crackled in the wind, tapping against the stones behind them. But it seemed to her that there was a moment when a black shadow passed before her in the blackness and that shortly after there was a disturbance among the bushes under the street light ahead. Her pursuer was now ahead of her and going farther away along the rim of the wall.

It was another twenty minutes before she began to move, as silently as she could, toward the gates. Her feet were awkward in the spaded and rigid borders, the cold had penetrated even the pit of her stomach. Romance and danger alike seemed unimportant beside the thought of a warm bed and limitless sleep. (Was courage, after all, only indifference?) Step by step she drew near the place where the wall bent to make the watchman's booth.

Then her toe caught on something lying across her path and she sprawled forward, scraping her hands on the rough ground, struggling to get her knees off the dreadful softness on which they had landed. Her hands groped, touched cloth, touched skin, encountered a stickiness like new paint.

Horror burst from her throat. She screamed and screamed, until Mr. Granahan came running out to put a hand over her mouth and still the senseless beating of her bloody hands against the empty air.

4

The morning newspapers, rearranging themselves hastily to give violence a front-page preference resorted to grim foreboding to cover up their paucity of facts.

AX MURDERER PROWLS
PHILADELPHIA SUBURBS

Body of Unknown Woman Found
Outside Stone Oaks Entrance

The body of an unidentified woman was discovered early this morning concealed in the shrubbery beside the gates of Stone Oaks, exclusive girls' school. James Granahan, night watchman for the school, reported the finding to the police after it had been seen by a Stone Oaks student who was returning late to the grounds.

The woman, about twenty-five years old, was fashionably dressed. There was only one head wound, but death had been instantaneous. Medical evidence is that the weapon was one with a sharp deep blade, probably a small ax. Walter Davis, police inspector assigned to the investigation, says that it is improbable that the murder was planned. "Only a miracle prevented the murderer from being caught in the very act," said Inspector Davis. "As it was, the body was found very shortly after the killing. If rape was intended, time must have prevented it. Except for the ax blow, there were no marks of violence on the body."

It is feared that this may be the work of a homicidal maniac and, as such, the first of a probable series of ax murders, according to Dr. Shallenbarger, city psychiatrist. "Ax murders are not common in our society," said Dr. Shallenbarger. "The use of such a primitive weapon is the mark of a savage nature which, in our civilization, denotes a man whose hand is against everyone, or a downright psychosis. It would be well for our citizens to employ caution in walking out at night, or in locking their doors until this killer is found."

There were reminiscences of the Cleveland torso murders. There were pictures of the dead woman, her face half-hidden by her black hair, her hat and purse thrown a little distance from her by the sharpness of her fall, her hands pathetically prominent in their expensive gloves. Many a woman reader held these pictures closer and studied, putting mental price tags on those beautiful clothes, and their sighs held a double regret—part for murder and part for beauty in the dust. As a woman columnist in another paper wrote:

The dead woman was undoubtedly a person of means and taste. The stunning combination of a rose-colored, short-sleeved wool dress with a slate-blue princess coat would not occur to most women; and the finding of suède pumps of the exact shade of the coat, and of a hat with a bit of ostrich plume the very color of the dress, could not have been easy. An ordinary woman, too, cannot afford a neckpiece made of six Hudson Bay sables, no matter how much she may admire that fur.

The women knew, even before the police, that here was a woman of consequence; and more than one of them, suppressing a twinge of envy, said to a neighbor that the killer might be a woman, basing this assumption on the inarticulated grounds that lovely and extravagant clothing does not endear one member of the feminine sex to another.

The afternoon editions furnished fresh ammunition for the bridge and tea tables. An autopsy had revealed that the dead woman was two months along in pregnancy, and feminine heads everywhere nodded wisely. It was her husband who had killed her, then. When the police discovered who she was and found the husband, they would have the murderer. This opinion, prompted by dark racial memories and founded on feeling rather than reason, was expressed without embarrassment by even those women who were most

59

happily married and who had the utmost confidence in their own mates. They could not have explained their automatic association between this wife's pregnancy and her husband's murderous reaction against it, but all their emotions told them that it was true.

By nightfall the papers had the facts, and public opinion was thrown into great confusion, for facts are the great unhappy rocks on which emotional convictions must shatter. The *Main-Liner's* story was typical, both in delicate inference and in significant omissions.

AX VICTIM IDENTIFIED AS
PROMINENT REAL ESTATE DEALER

Paternity of Felicia Waring's
Unborn Child a Mystery
to Her Family and Fiancé

The woman who was slain with an ax in the early morning hours outside the gates of Stone Oaks School for Girls has been identified as Felicia Waring, twenty-six, of New York City. The identification was made by her sister, Joan Waring, following publication of pictures in the morning press.

"I knew she had gone to Philadelphia for the week end on business," sobbed Joan, "but no one could have expected a thing like this to happen. She had many friends but no enemies."

Felicia and her sister Joan lived together in a Manhattan apartment, supported by their inheritance from their parents, the late Dr. Enoch and Olivia Waring. Joan, the younger, is in her last year at Columbia, and Felicia was the organizer and active head of the Bellhaven Real Estate Company. She belonged to several business women's associations and was generally respected as a fine executive type of young career woman.

The police can gather no information concerning the possible paternity of the unborn child revealed by the autopsy. Joan Waring had not been told of it by her sister; and Thomas Harper, the man who was to marry Felicia at Easter, professes ignorance. Mr. Harper is a Philadelphia resident, the son of Mr. and Mrs. Mark Harper, who are at present in Europe.

According to Joan, Felicia left a will, by which her estate will be divided between Joan and Mr. Harper, Felicia's fiancé.

The *Main-Liner* carried pictures of both Joan and Felicia Waring, and Annabelle Adams walked over to Alma House and up to Laura Derby's room with a copy of the paper in her hand. She did not seem displeased to find a group of four or five girls there, but she stood in the doorway and did not try to enter.

"Have any of you seen this picture of Felicia Waring?" she asked gently.

"What about it?" said Laura.

Annabelle smiled on them all. "Well, I kept looking at it and looking at it, and I knew it reminded me of someone, but I couldn't think who it might be." She thrust the paper at them. "Haven't any of you noticed the resemblance? My goodness, it's plain as can be, once you realize it. She looks like Dolores Kennedy, for all the world!"

The girls gathered around the paper, murmuring, and over their heads Laura and Annabelle confronted each other. "I suppose," said Laura, "that you'll feel it your duty to report your opinion to the police?"

"Oh yes," said Annabelle with great simplicity. "I think they ought to know. It may be important. What if the ax murderer killed the wrong woman, by mistake?"

"I'm pretty sure he did," Laura muttered balefully, but Annabelle was already going down the hall.

Mr. Granahan, ordinarily a stable and good-natured man, had turned confused and morose. Too many policemen looking at him queerly. Too many newspaper reporters clinging to him like bright-eyed leeches. He spoke to Miss Stone about the reporters and she performed a telephonic alchemy that made them disappear. The policemen kept coming, but by Monday their number seemed to have dwindled to one, a big plain-clothes man named Davis. And, at eight o'clock Tuesday morning, when Mr. Granahan left his booth by the Stone Oaks gates and walked to his little house on the edge of the grounds near the building that contained the school's heating plant, Davis was waiting for him on the front porch. Considering that the house was unlocked and the weather cold, it was damned nice of him to have stayed outside.

"Well!" Granahan said, almost cheerfully. "You must have got up before breakfast."

Davis waved a paper bag. "Brought breakfast with me," he said. "I wanted to catch you before you went to bed, and I thought it'd save time if we ate while we talked."

They sat in the warm kitchen and ate hamburgers and doughnuts, drank coffee from the cardboard containers, and Mr. Granahan was moved to tell of the huge indigestible meals he had eaten in odd places when he had been a fast passenger engineer for the New York Central. Davis listened so pleasantly that it was a shock when, as the doughnuts ended, he took out his notebook and opened it.

"Not again!" said Granahan, getting out his pipe. "A man gets tired talking about the same thing all the time."

"Just once more. They've put me in charge of the case, and I want to check the statements that were made before I came on it."

"I guess I can stand it if you can. Where'll we start?"

"At three o'clock at night. That was when you came back from a turn about the grounds and entered your booth?"

"Yes. I looked at my watch. It was three on the nose."

"Up until that time you had been aware of no disturbance whatever?"

"No. Everything was going just as usual."

"From midnight on you patrol the grounds once every hour?"

"Yes. Takes about forty minutes."

"And the rest of each hour you spend in the booth."

"Getting warmed up," explained Mr. Granahan. "I have a bad leg, stiffens up on me once in a while. The heat does it good."

"So. At three o'clock you sat down in the booth to eat your supper?"

"Coffee and sandwiches. I bring them along in my lunch box."

"The lights in the booth were on?"

"They're left on all the time at night."

Davis unfolded a paper. "Here's a drawing of the gates and the booth. Show me exactly where you sat to eat."

"Say, that's pretty slick," said Mr. Granahan interestedly. "You've got the street light and the sidewalk and everything."

"Concentrate on the booth," said Davis. "We'll come to the rest later."

"Well, there's the door to my booth, on the school side of the wall, just like you have it. I came in and closed it behind me. Then I pulled my chair over to the little table in front of the window."

"Facing the window?"

"Sure. Only way I can see the gates."

"The window was part-way open?"

"Yes. It's in the slant the wall takes there and the wind doesn't hit it, so I usually keep it open." He winked. "That way, if anybody tries to duck under the window and get by, I can hear 'em."

"The gates are kept locked after midnight?"

"That's right. Until twelve I'm in the booth all the time. Once I start making my rounds, the gates are locked."

"What if someone wants to get in while you're away?"

"They press the outside buzzer and that turns on little signal lights in three places on the grounds. When I see 'em, I hustle back to the entrance to let 'em in."

"Did anyone need to be admitted after midnight that Friday?"

"No."

"And you never patrol *outside* the wall. You're always inside it?"

"The city's supposed to take care of patrolling the outside," said Mr. Granahan slyly.

Davis smiled, but he did not look up from the drawing. "You ate supper, then, facing the half-open window. How long did you sit there?"

"Only a few minutes. I heard something out on the sidewalk, like a little scuffle. I pulled the window open farther and leaned out to see what was going on."

"And you saw nothing?"

"Not then. 'Probably the wind blowing the leaves,' I thought, and got ready to put the window down again. That was when I heard the second noise. It was a man's voice and it sounded like he was swearing."

"You're positive it was a man you heard?"

"Yes. Can't tell you what he said, though. It was just a word or two."

63

"What made you think he was swearing?"

"I don't know. Something about his tone of voice, I guess. Sort of like 'My God!' only there was a little more to it than that. It brought me right to my feet, I can tell you that!"

"You left the booth immediately?"

"Yes. I got out to the sidewalk as quick as I could."

"That means you had to leave the booth, walk along the inside of the wall, and let yourself out through the main gate."

"That's right. The whole thing doesn't take a minute."

"Now when you were outside on the walk. Did you lock the gates after you?"

"You bet I did. Learned my lesson long ago from a smart kid who was coming in mighty late. She had a bunch of her friends whoop it up a bit down the street, and when I stepped outside to see what was going on she slipped in the gate while my back was turned. Her house mother found out and gave me a talking to later. No sir! I locked those gates."

"And stood outside them looking around."

"Yep." He tapped the detective's sleeve with his pipe stem. "That was when I saw him. The murderer."

"You saw this man going by," corrected Davis. "Where was he when you first saw him?"

"He came out of the shadows the trees throw along there, and he didn't walk under the street light. He stayed out near the curb, where it's dimmer. Then he crossed the street and I couldn't see him any more. The trees are even thicker over there."

"All in all, how long a look did you get at him?"

"Ten seconds about. Not long enough to know him if I ever saw him again. He was going away pretty fast."

"But stumbling." Davis consulted his notebook. "Here's what you said before. 'Not walking exactly. Stumbling, like.'"

"Yes. Uncertain on his feet. Staggering a little." He gave up his struggle with the verbs of locomotion. "He was walking in a way that made me think he was drunk."

"He was a big man?"

"Bigger than I am. Powerful back he had."

"Could you make a guess as to how old a man he was?"

64

"Well, he wasn't stiff like an old man, and he wasn't limber like a kid. Twenty-some. Or forty. I don't know."

"Wearing a gray topcoat and hat?"

"Yep." His eyes brightened suddenly. " 'Lurchin', that's the word I want. He was lurching."

"And you followed him. Why?"

"Well, drunk or sick, he was a long way from home. That's open country over there, and I didn't want him getting run over on the highway or falling down asleep somewhere and catching the flu. Call it plain neighborliness, if you want to."

"But you didn't catch up with him?"

"No. I crossed the street and walked up and down a little, but I couldn't see him anywhere. So I went back to my booth and sat down again, wondering if I'd ought to call the precinct station and tell them there was a drunk loose. And I hadn't taken more'n one bite out of my sandwich until Miss Kennedy began to scream."

Davis closed his notebook. "The point at which the man came out of the shadows was near where the body was lying?"

"He couldn't have missed it," said Mr. Granahan. "Why, my God, when I walked out to cross the street, I was within fifteen paces of it myself!"

"And you're positive you could not identify that man if you were to see him again?"

"No sir, I wouldn't want to try it. One big fellow looks a lot like another big fellow by street light, and murder's too serious a thing to go making guesses about."

"It's doubtful if the man you saw was the murderer," said Davis mildly. "Miss Waring was killed sometime around midnight."

Mr. Granahan's jaw dropped. "You mean she was lying out there all that time? That anybody going by would have fallen right over her?"

"Yes. Unfortunately, no one seems to have gone by between eleven forty-five and three-fifteen."

Mr. Granahan closed his mouth and got his breath. "Well, if the man I saw wasn't the murderer, he at least saw the body there. Couldn't have helped it."

"Yes, he must have seen it."

65

Triumph lit Mr. Granahan's Irish face. "I told you there was something wrong about that guy! Why didn't *he* turn in the alarm?"

"That," said Davis, reaching for his hat, "is one of the things I intend to find out."

Inspector Davis made the décor of Miss Stone's living room seem ridiculous. It was a matter of proportion. Just as the frail and absurd dimensions of doll-house furniture become apparent when a child's hand reaches in to move it, so did the gilt chairs dwindle before masculine height and breadth. He sat on them without complaint and turned Miss Stone's thoughts to armchairs. Before the week was out she was driven to finding an English club chair in a corner of one of the students' lounges and having it moved into her rooms. Its heavy lines made the room appear to tip, gave her the lop-sided sensation of sliding downhill toward it, but her suffering was compensated when the inspector sat in it. Then the bulging thing became sturdily functional and the rest of the furniture trivial. Her imagination began to play with great sofas and wide wing-backed chairs, and when her watch bracelet inflicted a long scratch on the gilt desk top she sniffed and gave the desk a little kick for good measure.

But, except for polite considerations, they were enemies, for their purposes were at odds. It was the inspector's job to ferret out the truth without regard for consequences, to station one of his men outside Dolores's room in the infirmary, to haunt the place without regard for the damaging publicity his presence might give the school; and it was her concern to keep excitement down in the excitable student body and reassure the parents who behaved as if the man with the ax had been born and bred on Stone Oaks ground. They faced each other warily and with mutual reservations.

His first question each day was always the same. "How is Miss Kennedy?"

"Still in the oxygen tent. Dr. Leonard thinks that in another four or five days——"

He sighed. "Pneumonia's a pretty bad thing still, even if it isn't what it used to be. In this case, it's inconvenient besides. We can stop bothering you once we get to talk to her."

"I've sent for her father. He's coming tomorrow."

"I didn't know she was as sick as all that."

"There are other reasons for his coming." She looked down at the floor. "I think he ought to be present when you talk to her."

"Don't trust us very far, do you, Miss Stone?" he said regretfully.

"She's young and rather helpless. You could—and undoubtedly would—exclude me. I don't think you'll find it easy to exclude Mr. Kennedy."

He glanced at his notes. "You needn't threaten us with him. We've found out that he's a big shot, and I have my kid gloves all ready for him." From among his papers he pulled out a photograph. "You've seen this picture of Felicia Waring?"

"Yes. I believe it's the one the papers used."

"I haven't seen Miss Kennedy when she was conscious and well. One of your girls here says that there's a marked resemblance between her and the dead girl. I'd like your opinion."

"Which girl told you that?"

He cocked an eyebrow at her. "So there *is* a resemblance."

"A slight one. Both dark, both pretty, both about the same size."

"You couldn't go a little further than that?" She was silent, and he pulled his lower lip meditatively. "I'll be frank with you, Miss Stone. If the resemblance was strong enough so that one of them might have been mistaken for the other as she walked down the street, there's a chance that the ax murderer might have made a mistake."

"As long as the girl's dead," she said crisply, "I don't see that it matters whether he made a mistake or not."

"Oh yes, you do. Here are two girls from entirely different environments, having different groups of friends and acquaintances. One of them is killed. Now where do we look for the killer? In which group? If Miss Waring's death was intentional, we look among her associates. *But* if he intended to kill Miss Kennedy and made an error, then we must look among Miss Kennedy's acquaintances." He said slowly, "There's still the problem of why Miss

67

Waring was outside the Stone Oaks entrance in the first place. We have been able to discover nothing about that. She wasn't the sort to roam the streets by herself, especially at that hour of the morning. She must have had a reason. What was it?"

Miss Stone curled her lip. "Considering her physical condition——"

His interruption was gentle. "You mean the fact that she was pregnant?"

"Yes. Considering that, I'd say that you should look for a young man. There's a small woods half a mile from here, where—lovers—come to park every night. We've complained because it's not safe to have that sort of riffraff so close at peculiar hours of the night——"

"Riffraff? This girl wasn't riffraff, Miss Stone."

"Well, obviously she'd behaved in a cheap fashion, that's all I meant." Under his steady regard she flushed a little, became aware of her spinsterhood, stumbled over her own primness. "If her sister and her fiancé are really in the dark about the paternity of the child, then she must have met some man very secretly. I suggest that she met him that night—parked with him near the woods, perhaps—that they had some sort of disagreement that made her leave him, and that he overtook her later. We're the nearest place, she might have been running to us for shelter and couldn't make it in time."

He jotted down a note. "That could be. We'll look into it." He surveyed what he had written, tapping his pencil against his teeth. "There's a complication in that we have not been able to establish the exact time of death. It was a very cold night, the ground under her was frozen, she might as well have been lying in a refrigerator. We're certain that the killing took place sometime shortly after midnight, and that's as far as we can go. It makes things harder. We don't know just what time is important in the alibis we're getting, and the most ordinary alibi—the one of being asleep in bed—seems very reasonable, considering the time of night."

"I doubt if even Dolores will be able to tell you much. Unless" —she tried to make a joke of it—"unless she is under suspicion of having killed the girl herself."

68

"No," he said, "she wasn't the killer. The times don't jibe, nor her screaming, nor the disappearance of the weapon." He leaned toward her, making his point. "Moreover, Miss Stone, whoever did that job got some blood spattered on him. Make no mistake about that. Miss Kennedy had some blood on her hands, on the sleeve of her coat, and the edge of her skirt, but we didn't find any tiny splatters on her, and we would have if she'd done it." Unconsciously she sighed with relief, and he looked amused. "Now that you know that one of your chicks is safe, I'd like to speak to another one, please."

"Surely." She rose. "I'll send her in here to you. Which one do you want?"

"Miss Adams. Annabelle Adams."

She paused with her hand on the house phone. "She's the one who pointed out the likeness to you. Wasn't she?"

He grinned. "I'm not supposed to divulge my source of information, Miss Stone."

"Let me warn you that the Adams girl is a troublemaker. I regard her as one of our few mistakes. You can't place too much faith in anything she says."

"I'll say one thing in her favor," he said. "She's the only person around here who seems really anxious to talk."

"As long as you don't confuse willingness with accuracy," she said, and lifted the receiver.

Annabelle was having a good time. There was a flush of excitement on her high cheekbones and her thin lips were wet with saliva, as if she were drooling words. He had seldom seen a person in such a passion of hatred at the human race in general, she had nothing kind to say about anyone. Dolores Kennedy, according to Annabelle, was too high and mighty for her own good; and without reason, because everyone knew that her mother's family was peculiar, she had an uncle that was almost crazy. Yes, the uncle Dolores had been running up to New York to see. Winthrop Canby, his name was, but nobody could convince Annabelle that Dolores had made all those trips for *his* sake. She might fool Miss Stone, who was partial, anyway, to those girls whose families were the wealthiest; and she might mislead Mrs. Rhodes, who was, at best, an old idiot; but she didn't deceive Annabelle, not for a minute. Dolores had always meant to marry Richard Jordan, and, if she had to sleep with him to keep him in the meantime, she wasn't above doing it! (It occurred to the inspector that nowhere except in this society of pleasant, efficient schoolmistresses and carefully reared young women had he come across such a contempt for the normal physical phases of man.)

"I've met this Jordan boy," he said. "He hung around the infirmary all last Saturday and Sunday, and the nurse tells me that he telephones every day to see how his girl is getting along. Doesn't look to me as if Miss Kennedy had to worry about losing him."

"As far as I'm concerned, she can have him. He's conceited, too, so they'll make a fine pair. It just makes me sick to see how she pulls the wool over everybody's eyes, that's all. Miss Stone forbids her to go to New York any more, and she gets right up out of a sickbed and goes anyway. And what happens to her? Nothing. She's put back to bed and coddled and treated like royalty!"

Feminine spite always turned the inspector's stomach. He had been a widower for years now, but he could still recall the thin, sour voice of his erstwhile mother-in-law going on and on about the hatefulness of the world and the people in it. Being a patient man, he had never told the old woman that, when the whole world seemed foggy, it was often necessary only to wipe off your own windshield; and it was certainly not in his province to correct this young woman. Let her simmer in her own bile and eventually die wretched of it, as his mother-in-law had done. There was justice in the world beyond any that the police could bring about, he was convinced of that. In the last analysis, everyone was his own judge and his own executioner.

He broke into the long stream of general condemnation. "I take it you dislike Miss Kennedy," he said.

The light gray eyes wavered, showed a trace of alarm. "Not at all. I'm simply not fooled by her."

"That's evasive, Miss Adams. I'm hunting for some solid ground. Do you dislike her, or like her, or are you indifferent to her?"

"I don't see that my personal feelings matter."

70

"They matter very much. Naturally your evidence will be colored by your emotions."

"I am speaking as impersonally as possible."

The truth was not in her. He shifted to another tack. "What makes you think she went to New York that night? She hasn't been able to tell us where she'd been, you know. Were you in her confidence?"

"No, I——" She slipped to the edge of her chair and looked toward the door, and the inspector smiled to himself. She'd started something that she wished now she hadn't, but he wasn't going to let her off.

"She *told* you that she was going to New York?"

"Where else would she have gone?"

"Did you see her any time that night? Is that what makes you so sure?"

The alarm had turned into panic. She gasped, blinked, fluttered her hands aimlessly. "Of course I didn't see her. How in the world would I have seen her? I live in Rosemay Hall. Even if she had been at Alma House instead of the infirmary, I wouldn't have——"

"Your most intimate friends, then, live in Rosemay Hall?" It was absurd to imagine that this girl had any intimate friends, but he was after something.

"I know the Rosemay girls the best, yes. I wouldn't have bothered with Dolores at all if we weren't neighbors back home."

"You did not see her on Friday night at any time?"

"No."

"Your taxi called for you at eight-thirty and took you directly to the theater?"

"Yes."

"And brought you home immediately afterward?"

"Yes."

"When you reached here, you saw no one outside the wall on the sidewalk?"

"I've told you I didn't."

"You entered the gates and went at once to your room?"

"Yes."

The inspector shook his head wonderingly. "It seems strange to

71

me that a girl should set off on a bad night to see a play for which she had no ticket reservation and at an hour that insured her missing most of the first act."

"It was an impulse. 'One of Annabelle's notions,' my mother calls them." She shrugged. "Whatever the reason, I was there. Someone will remember me."

They had. In the omnipresent notebook was the corroborating evidence of two ushers and a member of the audience, but he did not tell her so. "And you were all alone the whole evening?"

"I'm usually alone."

She was more composed than she had been, and she wasn't saying a word she didn't have to. The inspector made his voice kind and paternal. "I don't know much about girls. Have two sons myself. I suppose you have a roommate, and that the two of you find the major part of companionship with each other and don't feel the need of much outside company. Girls don't seem to go in gangs, the way boys do."

"Third-year students have private rooms. Considering that my first- and second-year roommates were the worst that could have been chosen for me, I'm much happier by myself."

"Well, some people are more self-sufficient than others." He got to his feet. "I mustn't keep you here all day. Thanks for helping us."

She rose as a cobra rises from its coil, her tongue flicking out to moisten her lips. "I'm sorry I said what I did about Dolores. I mean the part about her sleeping with Richard. It wasn't very ladylike of me to mention it."

"Then why in the hell are you mentioning it twice?" thought the inspector. Aloud he said, "I discounted that on the grounds of your aversion to Miss Kennedy. It's not the sort of thing you could prove."

"I may not have proof, but I have my own reasons. Richard's one of them. I've never forgotten a time two years ago at a club dance back on River Island. I'd gone out on the veranda between dances to get cool, and he came out and kissed me in a perfectly loathsome way before I even knew what was happening!" She closed her eyes and shuddered, but it was the excessive moisture

72

on her lips that interested the inspector. "I gave him a piece of my mind, and he made some silly excuse or other, but I knew all I needed to know about him right then. I've given him a wide berth ever since, believe me."

"I see," said the inspector gravely.

She opened her eyes and smiled. "The other reason is a night-gown. A perfectly gorgeous one that Dolores didn't want me to see. She acted terribly strange about it. I wouldn't have been suspicious if she hadn't been so—furtive. And considering the passionate love story she'd turned in the week before to Miss Woods, the English mistress—well—I just put two and two together, that's all."

After she left, he jotted down some notes, his face crinkled with distaste. Then he reached for his hat, cast a longing look at the English club chair, and went to find Miss Stone.

Of Annabelle's two ex-roommates, only one was still in school. Her name was Phyllis Lovejoy, and when the inspector had tracked her to the library and signaled her out into the hall, she proved to be a small girl with bright eyes and a soft, fuzzy sweater. He extended his credentials to her in the manner of one holding out a nut to an unfamiliar squirrel, and she led him down the hall to a small room furnished with two chairs and a grand piano.

"Practice room," she said. "The music students have classes in the mornings, we'll be uninterrupted here." She took the smaller and more uncomfortable of the two chairs and looked at him alertly. "I'm tickled to death to have you get me away from the Napoleonic Wars, but honestly I don't know a thing that'll help you, Inspector. I was sound asleep that night at ten-thirty, darn it."

"I am interested in finding out all I can about a girl you know. Annabelle Adams."

Her dimples vanished, and she caught her lower lip momentarily between her teeth. "I don't know much about Annabelle, no more than anyone else does. She's a strange girl."

"Miss Stone tells me that you roomed with her for a year."

"Yes, I did. But we weren't particularly friendly."

"Still, you would know things about her that no one else would know. For instance, why she disliked Miss Kennedy."

She was watching him cautiously from beneath her eyelashes, like a small wild animal cornered in a hedge. "I don't know Miss Kennedy at all," she said.

"I'm not asking you to know Miss Kennedy. I'm asking you to know Miss Adams, and you do. Why are you afraid to talk about her?"

She laughed briefly. "People who talk about Annabelle get their comeuppance sooner or later. I'm not anxious to have her after my scalp." Even after he had pledged secrecy, she was reluctant. "When they find my suicide note a month from now," she said, "I hope it'll lie heavy on your conscience. Well, Annabelle hates everybody, but I think the reason she hated the Kennedy girl especially was that she was in love with the same man."

"Jordan?"

"That was his name. She didn't talk much about him, but she kept a picture of him buried in the bottom of her desk drawer. She showed it to me once, the first week we lived together, and when I asked who it was, she said it was a man back home who was terribly in love with her. And she simpered around and acted like a queen who was going to grant somebody a favor, but it was all a lie, of course. He never wrote to her, never telephoned, and after a while she didn't mention him any more. Instead, she began talking about Dolores Kennedy. Day and night she talked about her, couldn't get her off her mind. Dolores was sly and she was crazy and she was oversexed and heaven knows what all. I used to put a pillow over my head at night so I could get some sleep, and leave her droning on and on to herself."

"I don't know how you stood it," said the inspector honestly.

"I didn't stand it very well. I complained to the house mother and asked to have my room changed. I didn't mention Annabelle's obsession, I put it on the grounds that she snooped through my things, read my mail, listened in on my phone calls, tried to annex herself to my friends who wouldn't have her at any price. But it was a mistake for me to have asked, because there wasn't any other room to change to, and somehow Annabelle found out that I had complained. She turned quieter, and I was happy about that for a while. Then books I needed began to disappear and papers I'd

74

written ahead of time vanished just before I needed to turn them in. And I'd find out funny little rumors going around about me that couldn't be traced to any source but were the worst lies imaginable. I couldn't prove that Annabelle had started them, but who else would?" She shook off the recollection and smiled. "Maybe some girls would have had it out with her, but I'm a peace-at-any-price kind of person, and I knew darned well that I was no match for Annabelle. So I just gritted my teeth and stuck it out. Hard on my nervous system but wonderful for my character."

"Then, according to you, Miss Adams could not be considered a reliable witness?"

"I can't say that. She knows an awful lot, because she makes it her business to find out. I suspect she even follows some of the girls when they leave the grounds just to see where they've gone. I caught her climbing down the outside wall one time, and it was obvious that she'd been up there to spy on somebody, but I just said 'Good morning' and went right on. So she works like a beaver to satisfy her wicked curiosity, that much is true. But she also has an imagination, and I don't think that even Annabelle can tell where her facts end and her imagination begins."

A bell rang and she stood up. "Lunch!" she said. "I have to get my things out of the library before they lock it up. Want to come and eat with us? We're allowed to take guests."

"Thank you, no. I have to see Miss Stone again."

Her eyes twinkled. "So you're the reason she hasn't been in dining hall all week. We've wondered."

The inspector mused, as he plodded back to the administration building, that he was a person Stone Oaks could get along without on two counts: first, he was a man, a species that the whole place was geared to exclude; second, he was a detective, and they were used to doing their own detecting. It pained him to realize that, with their sharp eyes and womanish guesses, these girls were making an everyday diversion out of what to him was a painstaking profession. Whoever had first thought up the idea of locking a bunch of mature and semi-mature women up together had been an enemy to society! What this place needed was an avalanche of fathers and brothers and healthy young men with loud voices and heels that hit pavement firmly and were hell on rugs and female me-grims. These women, blocked of normal outlet, were feeding on one another as a matter of course. He was going to have his hands full seeing that they didn't eat him too.

It was Saturday when they told him he could talk to the Ken-nedy girl, and he was ready. In his pocket was the small fragment of paper with her handwriting on it that had been inexplicably found caught in the zipper of the dead woman's purse. In his files was the testimony of the ticket agent at the Philadelphia station who had sold her a round-trip ticket that Friday night. That was all he had, and he must rely on the girl's good will for the rest of what he wanted. Since she could not have killed Felicia Waring, nor been present at the killing, there was no pressure that could be brought to bear on her. Patiently the night before he had made this clear to a city official so powerful that the inspector made a habit of thinking of him as Mr. X, lest by mistake he should let the real name slip at an inopportune time.

"Listen, Walt," Mr. X had said at last, "this Stone Oaks business is bad enough. Hell, my wife's on the board of trustees. But Bob Kennedy's a national figure, president of one of the biggest insur-ance companies in the world. It's ridiculous to suppose that his daughter is implicated in this thing beyond having the bad luck to stumble over the body."

"We're not worried about implication," said the inspector. "There's a chance that somebody was after Miss Kennedy and got Felicia Waring by mistake. I think we should go into that possi-bility rather thoroughly, for Miss Kennedy's future safety if for nothing else."

Mr. X cleared his throat. "Put it to Bob Kennedy on that basis right off then, Walt. I don't want him to get huffy, and if he realizes that you're primarily concerned with his daughter's wel-fare——"

"I'm concerned with the public welfare and Miss Kennedy is part of the public. I'll make him see that, if he doesn't already know it."

"For God's sake!" roared Mr. X. "Quit joking. Haven't you ever

76

heard about special privilege? Wait till you meet him, you'll see what I mean."

As it happened, the inspector had already met Mr. Kennedy, briefly, in Miss Stone's office, and had sized him up as one of those rare men who combine culture and hard business sense to a degree where they become indomitable, being able to get their own way by charm or by force with equal facility. Mr. Kennedy had all the equipment for being memorable: an excellent carriage, a handsome head, good hands, and a fine voice. But under his overlay of good manners he had a self-confidence so superb that it got under the inspector's skin. The reverse side of knowing oneself to be wonderful was a contempt for the rest of the human race—a contempt which the inspector could not share and hence resented.

He went to the infirmary that morning in a bad, aggressive mood, which was not improved by having to sit in a chair in the reception room until Dr. Leonard was through with the patient. As if he didn't have Thomas Harper, the dead woman's fiancé, coming to his office at eleven o'clock and showing every sign of being a tough nut to crack! He fumed, thinking about Harper and possible ways to break Harper's alibi, until Mr. Kennedy came striding out to him.

"Sorry to make you wait, Inspector Davis," said Mr. Kennedy, for all the world as if he meant it. "The doctor'll only be a few minutes longer." He sat down in the chair by the inspector's elbow. "He says I can take her home in a few more days, thank God. Her mother's not well and nearly crazy with worry by this time, and Dolores isn't acting much like herself. I'll be glad to get the two of them together and sit down."

"I didn't know you were taking her home."

Mr. Kennedy looked down at his hands. "There's no help for it. She's been expelled."

"Miss Stone didn't tell me."

"She's doing us the favor of not making it public. We can say it's because Dolores isn't well, but actually it's because she broke about every rule in the place that night." He looked less of a divinity now, with the worriment in his eyes and mouth and the daylight glinting on the white in his dark hair. "I don't blame the school. They have to have their regulations. But I can't understand Dolores. She's always been a sweet, quiet little thing, and then to have her go off on an unreasonable tangent like that——"

The inspector thawed. "It may look a lot worse than it is. Have you talked to her?"

"A little. She says she had to go up to New York to see her uncle, Winthrop Canby. Doesn't know why, just felt she had to see him. And it wasn't until she was riding a bus through the city that she remembered he wouldn't be there, he'd already gone to Florida. So she turned around and took the next train back. The last part of the trip she doesn't remember very well. Her temperature was a hundred and four when she was put back to bed, so that's understandable. I keep hoping that it was the fever that sent her off on that wild-goose chase in the first place. No rational person would ever regard Winthrop as a haven of refuge, that much I'm sure of."

"If she'd said that she made the trip to see Richard Jordan," said the inspector slowly, "it would be easier to believe. But he wasn't there. He was in Philadelphia, ready to come out and visit her the next morning."

Mr. Kennedy proffered a cigar and held a lighter. "Still, he was in Philadelphia. You don't suppose he could be mixed up in this affair some way?"

The inspector resisted the impulse to turn his head sharply. He puffed at his cigar and felt the strain of keeping his neck muscles still. "So far our evidence shows no connection between him and the dead woman. Of course we're not through by a long sight."

"Naturally I hope he isn't involved," said Mr. Kennedy hastily. "Dolores is very fond of the boy."

The inspector did not have to ask whether Mr. Kennedy liked "the boy." He already knew the answer to that.

She gave her story quietly, with her father holding her hand from one side of the bed and the inspector taking notes on the other. Gently he led her back over every step of the evening, marking traintimes, eliciting a description of the cab that had brought her out to Stone Oaks. As he had guessed, it was an independent cab, which was why they had not yet located the driver.

78

"You were going to have to enter the grounds secretly. How did you plan to do that?"

"I hadn't thought that far. I guess I was going to wait until Mr. Granahan was off on the grounds and then try to get over the gates." She stirred, as if she had become suddenly uncomfortable. "I couldn't think very well. Someone was following me and I was frightened."

The inspector leaned forward, too intent for note-taking. "When did you first notice that someone was following you?"

"I'm not clear about that. While I was trying to get a cab to bring me here, maybe. But I wasn't sure of it until I started to walk the last few blocks. I hid in the bushes until whoever it was had gone by."

"You didn't see who it was?"

"No, I couldn't see anything." For the first time she turned her full face toward him, and he could see the childish bewilderment on it. "It must have been the murderer, mustn't it?"

"If it was, he'd already killed one girl and come back for another. Miss Waring was dead before you got off the train in Philadelphia."

"How queer," she said softly. "I had it figured out a different way. When I fell over her, I thought it must have happened only a few minutes before."

"She hasn't seen the papers," said Mr. Kennedy warningly, "and we've tried to keep her from thinking about it."

"I see," said the inspector. "Did you know Felicia Waring, Miss Kennedy?"

"No."

"You have never written a letter—perhaps a business letter—to any person by that name?"

"No. I never heard the name until I asked who it was that——"

He brought out the scrap of paper. "Is this your handwriting?"

A faint color came into her pale cheeks. "Yes, I think it is."

"We haven't been able to find the page from which this was torn. Can you tell us what that page contained?"

"There were several pages. This is from the first draft of a theme I wrote for English class some weeks ago. Miss Woods has the copy if you want to see it."

79

"What became of that first draft?"

"I lost it. It was in my purse, and then, when I went to look for it, it wasn't."

"Your name was on it?"

"My name and the date and the number of my English section." Her voice trembled. "Why? Is it important?

"We found this piece of it in Miss Waring's purse. It was caught in the zipper, as if the rest had been wrenched away."

"Perhaps Miss Waring found it," said Mr. Kennedy, "and was coming to return it."

"At midnight?" From his breast pocket he produced a photograph and gave it to Dolores. "This was Miss Waring. To the best of your knowledge, have you ever seen her before?"

"No," she said. "I don't think I——" She hesitated, moving her hands over the picture, blocking out the hair so that only the face was left. "It's the girl on the train," she said weakly, and leaned back against the pillow and closed her eyes.

The inspector prayed that her strength would hold out, and it did. In little gasps she told about the loss of her purse and its return. No, she had not missed the paper then, she had not been thinking about the paper. Yes, Miss Waring had had time to take it, if she'd wanted to. No, Dolores had not seen her again, not even in the exodus from the train.

"There is no reason to believe that she was not on the train by coincidence? That she might have been following you?"

The soft eyes came up to his in innocent bewilderment. "But it was a man who was following me that night," she said simply.

A surprised oath exploded in the inspector's mind, but he kept his demeanor calm. "That was exactly two weeks previous to the murder?"

"Yes. On a Friday evening."

He went over that exhaustively, but there was not much in it. "You're positive you did not recognize the man in the other taxi?"

"No. I didn't see his face."

"Big man? Small man?"

She said, hesitantly, "His shoulders were big. Or perhaps his overcoat was padded. Anyway, he seemed big."

80

"What color was the overcoat?"

"Gray, I think. The hat was too."

Mr. Kennedy looked outraged. "If anything like that happens again, Dolores, you are to call the police at once. I can't imagine why Winthrop didn't call them!"

She turned her head on the pillow. "I didn't tell Uncle Win. I didn't tell anyone. You see, I thought it was all a mistake, and I——"

"It may have been a mistake," said Inspector Davis. "You've never had anything like that happen to you before?"

"No. No, never." Her hands began to move restlessly on the counterpane, and her voice was weaker. "I'm not even sure that it happened then."

He saw that he must not tax her further, and he spoke quickly. "At any time on the night of the murder did you see a big man wearing a gray topcoat and hat?"

"There must have been lots of them. I didn't notice."

"But near you? Conspicuously where you were?"

"No, not that I——" Her voice stopped, and her eyes widened, staring at the wall. "A man like that passed me, but he didn't even look at me. He ran down the stairs while I was——"

"While you were—what?"

In the silence there was only the sound of her breathing, quick and light. Then she covered her face with her hands. "I'm going crazy," she whispered. "I didn't see anyone that night. No one at all."

"Don't fret about it, honey," said her father. "It's all over and I'm right here to look after you." But, out in the hall once more, he wiped his upper lip with his handkerchief and sighed. "She's weaker than you'd think. Odd about that scrap of paper, isn't it?"

"The oddest thing about this whole case," said the inspector, "is that the two girls looked like each other. If Miss Waring had been a six-foot redhead, a lot of my problems would be solved."

"What are you talking about?" said Mr. Kennedy with a trace of irritation. "That girl looked no more like Dolores than a chunk of granite looks like a piece of marble."

The outside door opened then, and Richard Jordan came in,

turning down his coat collar. "Good morning," he said cheerfully. "Visitors in order today?" He went directly into Dolores's room and they heard her soft exclamation of his name.

Mr. Kennedy's face grew stern. "Where's the nurse? She ought to be here to tell him not to stay long. Dolores is upset enough as it is." He reached for the inspector's hand and shook it absent-mindedly. "Good-by, sir. I feel that the case couldn't be in better hands. I've already said as much to some rather influential friends of mine here."

As he walked to his car, the inspector brooded over the threat that lay in those "influential friends." What Mr. Kennedy was saying, in effect, was, "As long as you don't bother us too much, Davis, I'm willing to show my appreciation where it counts. Make a nuisance of yourself and I have ways of getting even." His lip curled as he put the car into gear and headed for his office and Thomas Harper, who probably had influential friends too.

Three weeks later, just at the hour of the evening when Mr. Granahan came on duty, a police car parked in front of the main entrance and Inspector Davis rapped on the window of the booth and signaled Mr. Granahan outside.

"You want to come in?" asked Mr. Granahan, joining him.

"No. We just brought somebody out to look the situation over." He made a vague gesture toward the curb, where two police officers in uniform were walking about, the street light winking on badges and buttons and polished belts. They had a man in ordinary clothes with them, a big fellow in a dark overcoat and hat.

Mr. Granahan watched. "What're they supposed to be doing?"

"They're pointing out the spot where the body was found, I think."

"Well, hell, they're showing him the wrong place! It was down the walk about fifteen feet."

"They know it," said Davis. "They want to see if he knows it."

The man in civilian clothes stood with his back to the gates, looking dutifully down at the place the officers had indicated. And as the little group moved back and forth in the lighted area that formed Mr. Granahan's nightly stage, the watchman shifted his feet and glanced out of the corner of his eye at the immobile Davis.

"Do I know that fellow?" he asked suspiciously.

"I don't think so."

Mr. Granahan rubbed his chin. "Seems familiar, somehow."

"I hoped he would."

"Oh," said Mr. Granahan, enlightened. Then, reproachfully, "You might have told me what you wanted in the first place."

"I didn't want to influence you."

"Who is he?"

"Name's Thomas Harper. He's an attorney here in town."

"Like I told you," said Mr. Granahan, "I'm in no position to say for sure. The guy I saw that night was the same size and build. That's as far as I can go. If this Harper was staggering and had on a gray overcoat, he'd be a dead ringer for him. So would a lot of other guys."

"Harper says he doesn't own a gray overcoat," said Davis softly. "Had one up until a few weeks ago and gave it to the Salvation Army, he says. Well, thanks very much."

"Not a-tall," said Mr. Granahan.

He watched them all pile back into the car, and he noticed that Harper, at the last minute, turned his head and looked down the street in the direction where the body had really been. Didn't mean much, might have been accidental. But it had been a bad thing for Harper to do, with the inspector's eyes within twelve inches of the back of his neck.

5

River Island was a snowdrift set in wide aisles of glass with only a few dark splinters far out from the shore to show that the powerful current still churned below. From her bed, covered by white sheets and white eiderdown, Dolores watched without interest the pageantry of winter framed by her window: the children skating on the safely frozen edges; the snowplows clearing the River Road; and, at Christmastime, the Reeses' sleigh jingling up the driveway to leave the traditional box of holly at the door. Her mother and father sat beside her for hours, and now and then a neighbor visited her; but, though she tried to smile or nod or shake her head as the situation might demand, nothing was important to her, she lived among mirages. Each day began fresh, unstained by any recollection of the day before, and she was empty and content.

Dr. Crooke, the family physician, said that it was a case of nervous exhaustion, that with rest and proper diet she would change. "You're in a state of suspended animation," he said. "Don't confuse it with being alive."

"I am happier now than I have been for months."

That displeased him. "Happy to be weak and in bed and out of things? That shows how sick you really are!"

By day there were letters and by night there were her dreams, and both affected her as slightly as a faint knock on a distant door affects a heavy sleeper who has no intention of breaking his rest to answer. Laura's letters had clippings in them, and these she unfolded and read dutifully, throwing them away immediately afterward, vague ten minutes later about what they had said. Only one of them punched its way momentarily through her listlessness: FIANCÉ OF DAUGHTER TO KENNEDY FORTUNE ADMITS KNOWING AX VICTIM, "Met Her at College Dance," Jordan Says. Laura's accompanying letter was indignant. "This is one of those horrible implications that newspapers use to make a spectacular front page," she wrote. "You'll notice, a long way down in the small print, that Richard was introduced to her, danced with her once, and never saw her again. I made a protest to Inspector Davis—he still comes around occasionally—about such an item being given to the press for the sake of a Roman holiday, and he said that, while the information was correct, he had not been the one to divulge it."

Richard's letters contained no reference to the police or to Felicia Waring. He joked about a warning he had had from the dean—"who told me that, if I were having exceptional difficulty, I should hire a tutor, and it was plain to see that he pitied my stupidity rather than condemned it. I almost told him that he was in the presence of genius, because I had maintained a D rating without opening the books at all. But I am studying now like a good, good boy." At Christmastime he sent her, from New Orleans, a box of pralines, an airy stole of intricate hand-made lace, and an ancient and beautiful painted fan. "Save the shawl and the fan to wear when we come here on our honeymoon. You will be the most beautiful thing in this beautiful city." She let her mother put the lace away in a satin case; the fan she kept on the bed table beside her. Often she opened it to look at the bowing, smiling figures with the little Loves circling around their heads, but she did not think of Richard nor long for him. Sometimes she closed her eyes and tried to reinvoke his image, but no picture came. She saw only the grayness of daylight filtering through her eyelids, and, in a few seconds, she slept.

Among the dimly disturbing dreams there was a recurring one so real that, the first time, she had not known it was a dream. She had thought herself lying awake in the night watching the shadows the moon cast into her room; and it seemed to her that her father came in with a flashlight in his hand, looking for her. When the circle of brilliance fell on her face, she threw a protecting hand over her eyes and heard him say, triumphantly, "Oh, *there* you are!" Since she wakened immediately and turned on her bed lamp to find the room empty, she knew the little incident could not have happened. Still, she asked her father the next day if he had been prowling the house with a flashlight. He had not, of course. And when the dream returned, it was not her father who held the flashlight, but Richard; and another time it was someone whom she did not know, a man in a light gray overcoat with a hat pulled down over his eyes.

Except for dining with one of his sons on Thanksgiving and with the other on Christmas, Inspector Davis paid no attention to holidays. At eight o'clock on the morning of New Year's Day he walked into his office, inserted a new pad in his desk calendar, and sat down behind his battery of telephones. It would be a busy day, and he would sit there for sixteen hours, having added Inspector MacPherson's trick to his own. ("You'll be doing not only myself, but the department, a favor," MacPherson always said. "For what good could I possibly be to the force on New Year's Day in the condition I'll be in!") From outside his door he could hear the teletype pounding away and typewriters clicking; and from far below him came the noise of motors and the clanging of the doors of the police garage, which took up the entire street floor. The inspector heard none of it. He had acquired the habit of working uninterruptedly, amidst interruptions.

And today he had something to work on. Five gray buttons made of bone. Five gray buttons of the size used on men's overcoats, with bits of ash and charred thread clinging to them. The first solid bit of luck he'd had in the Felicia Waring case.

He turned the pages of Officer Weir's report, which had come in with the buttons:

I took up my station in the alley back of the Harper house at four o'clock in the afternoon, relieving White. While it was daylight I kept out of sight of the house, but always where I could see the trash burner. It's a big metal drum with holes punched here and there to give it a draft, and it sits just inside the Harpers' alley gate. At eight o'clock, as usual, the housekeeper came out with a wastebasket full of papers which she burned. As soon as the ashes were cool, I sifted them but found nothing. About eleven o'clock the back porch light came on and Thomas Harper came out with a bundle in his arms wrapped in newspaper. He dumped this into the trash burner, set a match to it, and stood there for ten minutes watching it burn. Shortly before midnight I went through the ashes again and found the buttons. When Henderson came to relieve me, we located some old bushel baskets and emptied the contents of the trash burner into them. A squad car picked them up for us and said they would deliver them to the laboratory.

The inspector had already established that the lab report would be ready by three o'clock. For the hundredth time he took out the Waring file and tried to work out a timetable for the night of November 11 that would make sense.

7:30
Miss Waring takes her car out of its garage in New York, asking if the tank is full enough for a run to Philadelphia. She is alone and dressed in the same clothes in which she was later found. (Evidence of garage attendant.)
10:30
She parks her car in the Sure-Way Garage in Philadelphia, saying that she will not need it again till morning. She is alone, but one of the garage men is under the impression that, before she drove in, she let a man out on the sidewalk and that he was waiting out there for Miss Waring to rejoin him.

(Two things wrong so far. Unless Miss Waring had driven very slowly, it would not have taken her three hours to make that trip. Consequently, she must have spent some of the time somewhere else. Picking up the man, maybe? And, if the man were Harper, wouldn't she have thought it strange that he had waited outside the garage for her?)

10:45
Miss Waring and an unidentified man go into Gus Linke's diner and order coffee. They sit in a booth and Gus says that the girl was angry. (Gus is not a reliable witness. After looking at photographs, he *thinks*

the girl was Miss Waring and he admits not noticing the man at all. However, Carol Jamison, a girl who sat at a table near the door, was able to describe Miss Waring's costume to the last detail, so it is probable that Miss Waring was there. Miss Jamison also has no evidence concerning the man. "A big fellow," she says. But it turns out that, to Miss Jamison, a man five feet ten inches tall is "big.")

11:00
Miss Waring boards a bus that takes her to a corner near the school gates. (Evidence of Mrs. Benjamin Ezekiel, fellow passenger. Mr. Ezekiel is a furrier and Mrs. Ezekiel's attention was attracted by Miss Waring's sables. She had no conversation with Miss Waring but thought it unusual that so well dressed and pretty a young woman should be traveling alone by bus at night.)

And that was all. At twelve-five Miss Waring had left the bus at one of its regular suburban stops, her last mortal act for which there was any proof.

He turned the pages to Thomas Harper's testimony, which was equally unsatisfactory. It began with Harper's statement that he had planned to go up to New York and take Miss Waring to dinner and a show that evening, but she had called him in the afternoon to break the date on the grounds that she had a business appointment.

Q. She called you at your office?
A. No. I had just reached home. It was about six in the evening.
Q. Wasn't it unusual for her to break a date at such short notice?
A. I wouldn't say so. She had done it before on occasion.
Q. She told you she was coming down to Philadelphia that night?
A. Yes. She said there were people she had to see, but if it didn't get too late she might call me afterward.
Q. And you accepted that without question?
A. Well, I tried to find out where she'd be, thinking I might meet her somewhere, but she said nothing was definite. She had several errands—to see someone downtown and then perhaps to go out to Stone Oaks.
Q. She said plainly that she intended to visit Stone Oaks?
A. I got the idea that she thought she might not have to go out there if other things worked out right.
Q. You knew where the school was?

88

A. Yes. I had a cousin who was enrolled there some years ago.

Q. You yourself have never been there?

A. No.

Q. How long had you and Miss Waring been engaged?

A. For almost a year.

Q. You had known her before that?

A. From the time I was in grade school. The Waring family lived here then. They moved to New York when I was in my first year at high school and I lost track of them.

Q. Until a year ago?

A. Closer to eighteen months, perhaps. I ran into Joan in a New York restaurant one day. She told me that her parents were dead and that she and her sister were living together in an apartment. I went there for dinner two nights later.

Q. And subsequently became engaged to Felicia?

A. Yes.

Q. You gave her an engagement ring?

A. Yes. She chose it herself. It was a circlet of emeralds and diamonds.

Q. Was she in the habit of wearing it constantly?

A. There may have been times when she did not wear it. I don't know.

Q. She was always wearing it when you were with her?

A. (Pause.) Yes.

Q. She was not wearing the ring on the night she was murdered.

A. So I understand.

Q. She had left it in her jewel box at home. Can you account for that?

A. No.

Q. The two of you had not quarreled?

A. No.

Q. The engagement had not been broken?

A. No.

Q. When you were first engaged, how often did you see her?

A. Two or three times a week, I suppose.

Q. How often had you seen her in the last month?

A. That's hardly a fair comparison. This is a very busy time of year for me and Felicia was involved in a long-drawn-out business about somebody's estate——

Q. How often had you seen her in the last month?

A. Two or three times. I don't know. I spoke to her frequently by telephone.

Q. Had she broken other dates with you?

A. Yes. She was a businesswoman. Matters would arise that took precedence over her personal affairs.

Q. You had no suspicion that she might have fallen in love with another man?

A. (*Pause.*) She did not tell me that she had.

Q. You think she would have told you, had that been the case?

A. There would have been no reason why she should not tell me.

Q. But she did not?

A. No. (*Pause.*) It's obvious to me now that there must have been another man.

(Harper had seen the danger there. In the midst of protesting that there had been no quarrel between Felicia and himself he had realized that there was the fact of her pregnancy to be accounted for.)

Q. I am going to put a hypothetical question to you, Mr. Harper. You need not answer it.

A. I will answer it if I can.

Q. If Miss Waring had told you that she was about to have a child, would you still have married her?

A. She would not have wished me to. If she were enough in love with another man to have a child by him, then she would not have wanted to marry me.

Q. According to that, you must believe that she was *not* in love with you.

A. I believe now that she was not.

Q. But on the night of November 11 you believed that she was?

A. Yes. She had seemed distracted for the past several months but I put that down to business worries, as I told you.

Q. You were alone in the house when she telephoned you that evening?

A. Yes. Since my parents went to England in September, a cleaning woman comes one day a week, but it is usually on Mondays. I take my meals out.

Q. Rather a lonely life for you.

A. I have a great many friends. I can find companionship whenever I want it.

Q. After the phone call, what did you do?

A. I went downtown to have dinner at the Red Raven.

Q. You had just come from downtown and you went back immediately?

A. Well, my plans had changed.

Q. You dined alone?

A. Yes. Oh, Bill Collins came in just as I was finishing and he sat at my table for a while.

Q. Mr. Collins is a good friend of yours?

A. Not exactly. He's a business acquaintance whom I happen to like.

Q. When did you leave the restaurant?

A. About eight forty-five.

Q. Approximately or definitely?

A. Definitely. It was looking at my watch that gave me the notion of going to the railroad terminal. A train from New York comes in there at nine.

Q. And you thought Miss Waring might be on that train?

A. It was one she had taken before. I thought it barely possible.

Q. You had something you wanted to say to her?

A. No. I didn't have anything better to do and—well, it would have been nice to see her for a few minutes. At that time I didn't know she had decided to drive down, of course.

Q. You arrived at the terminal about nine. How long did you stay there?

A. About an hour and a half. Until I was sure that somehow I had missed her.

Q. Did you speak to anyone while you were there? Run into anyone you know?

A. No.

Q. There is a train leaving Philadelphia for New York shortly after nine-thirty. You did not take it?

A. That's a peculiar question. I had no reason to want to go to New York.

Q. Did you hear that train called while you were there?

A. I may have. I don't remember.

Q. What did you do after you left the station?

A. I took a bus home and went to bed.

Q. Without waiting for the late call Miss Waring had half-promised to make?

A. There was no need to. I have a phone beside my bed.

Q. You have a car, Mr. Harper?

A. Yes. I don't use it much. Transportation in our area is very good.

Q. On the night of November 11 your car was never out of the garage?

A. No.

Q. Thank you very much. If we need to talk to you again, we will be able to reach you at your present address?

A. Yes.

The inspector laid a hand on the telephone and took it away again. No, he didn't want to talk to Thomas Harper today. Let the young man discover the empty trash burner and wonder; give him time to develop a state of nerves. He'd be a good bit easier to talk to after that.

With the slowly lengthening days of February, Dr. Crooke insisted that Dolores spend a part of each sunny day in the garden. They set a chair for her beside a high, protecting wall and there she sat, blanket-wrapped and indignant, counting the minutes until she would be permitted to go back to her room again. Protestations did her no good at all.

"I'm not ill any longer," she said. "If I prefer to stay in the house, what harm is there in that?"

"So you're not ill."

"Not now."

"A patient's diagnosis of his own case is always interesting, but I think you'd do better to abide by a doctor's opinion."

"I had so many plans for my life," she said, "and they all exploded in my face at once. I'm not anxious to build them up again. Is that sickness? Can you cure it?"

"Yes, that's sickness," said Dr. Crooke angrily, "and I can't cure it. But you can."

So it was in the snow-covered garden that she sat to read the clippings that Laura sent on.

POLICE HUNT MYSTERY MAN IN WARING CASE AS SENIOR HARPERS RETURN FROM EUROPE. WHO WAS FATHER OF FELICIA'S UNBORN CHILD? POLICE SEARCH IS FRUITLESS. RESTAURANT PROPRIETOR IDENTIFIES HARPER AS MAN WHO DINED WITH FELICIA ON MURDER NIGHT. HARPER'S ALIBI

BROKEN: "OUT IN HIS CAR THAT NIGHT" NEIGHBOR SAYS.

Nowhere did there appear an explanation of why Felicia had been at the gates of Stone Oaks in the middle of a winter's night. Dolores herself had turned into "young student, returning late from Friday privilege," and remained nameless. She observed these details without wonder, walking carefully past the frozen peony hedge to heap the reports on the grille of the outdoor fireplace and to set a match to them. "Listen!" wrote Laura with spirit. "If I'm wasting my time sending you this stuff, let me know. I spend hours getting it together for you and I don't believe you even read it, ungrateful creature." She answered politely, "I read it. Thank you, Laura."

She was beginning to be afraid of the garden. The weak sun and the scudding wind; the tangle of blue jays and cardinals around the feeding station; the gray line of flowing water in the middle of the frozen river; the lights and half-lights of the winter sky; these infected her with their color and mood and motion in spite of herself. The brisk air swept her dreaminess away and slapped her painfully alive. Gradually her father and mother changed from half-acknowledged presences into individuals, anxious and loving; and Laura and Richard, Annabelle and Uncle Win, were no longer names, but people with roundness and meaning. It fretted her that the meaning was so often unpleasant.

"How are you today?" said the doctor.

"Miserable," she answered promptly. "Miserable and unhappy and not up to doing anything about it."

He laughed. "A stranger and afraid in a world you never made? That's fine. That's more like it. Now how about asking some youngsters to drop in and cheer you up?"

"The ones I know best are away at school."

"Then try somebody you don't know very well. How about young Lansing? He's a good-looking young fellow, might take you dancing at the Yacht Club, if you'd inkle."

"I'm engaged. I don't think I'm supposed to inkle."

"But I thought——" he began gruffly, and fell into an embarrassed silence.

93

When he had gone, she lay back frowning. If Dr. Crooke had sensed that she was no longer in love with Richard, then, in all fairness, Richard should know it too. Somewhere in the last few months she had changed from the frantic, passionate creature who had stumbled through the streets of two cities to find him; and the quiet, subdued girl that she was now looked on him, not as a god, but as a handsome young man around whom she had built romantic air castles that time and distance had tumbled down.

The garden paths had been shoveled clear, especially for her, and she went walking on them, lifting her face to the wind, catching snowflakes in her mittened hands. There was no logical way of telling a young man that, without his doing a thing to warrant it, you had fallen out of love with him. The sentences that formed in her mind were silly and unsuitable, and she was greatly tempted not to write to him at all. But her conscience would not permit that. In the end, she scribbled a note to him—she was never certain of what she had written—and sent it off. For better or for worse, she had at last faced a situation and made a decision.

In March she made her re-entrance into Island affairs by accepting an invitation to accompany her parents to a dinner that the Florians were giving. Like all the Florian affairs, it would be extremely formal, and for the first time in months she took great care in dressing. Ruffled chiffon and pearls, gloves, and painted fan. Her reflection in the mirror gave her pleasure and, as she crossed the hall to her mother's room, she sang softly to herself. "Black Is the Color of My True Love's Hair." But I have no true love, she thought as she sang; it may be that I am not capable of true love.

Mrs. Kennedy was sitting on the vanity bench before her mirror, her amber satin gown still unfastened, her head bowed forward on her clenched hands. In one startled second Dolores took in the pallor, the slight grimace of pain, the patient anguish of the body; and, even in her alarm, she moved slowly and quietly, so apparent was it that this waxen woman must be protected from the vigors of the living. "Are you ill, Mother? What's the matter, darling?"

At once her mother's shoulders straightened and she turned, smiling, touching the white chiffon ruffles of her daughter's dress.

"How pretty," she said. "It's good to see you looking like a young girl again."

"If you don't feel up to going, Mother——"

"Nonsense. A little headache. I'll be all right." She allowed Dolores to fasten her dress, find her a handkerchief, unlock the jewel cases. "I'll finish by myself, dear. Go on down to your father and tell him I'll be right along. You know how impatient he gets."

It was a convincing performance, but Dolores was not deceived. She cried when she reported to her father what she had seen, and he set his cocktail glass down somberly and offered her his handkerchief. "I know," he said. "I've talked myself hoarse, but she won't see a doctor."

"The dress," she said tearfully. "It fit her two weeks ago when she bought it and now it hangs on her. Why didn't you tell me she was so sick? I should have been told."

"But I did tell you. I wrote it to you last year, just before Thanksgiving."

Between self-reproach and terror her voice was a whisper. "I didn't realize. I was crazy then. And ever since I've been so busy thinking of myself that I took everything else for granted. While I lay in bed pitying myself, she was dying on her feet!"

"Don't say that, Dolores. My God, it can't be that bad."

She wanted to protest that it was, it *was* that bad, but she caught herself in time. She perceived that he was even less prepared for this tragedy than she, and she wiped her eyes quickly and assumed an optimistic air. "We'll find out," she said. "She's going to the hospital for a check-up tomorrow if I have to drag her every step of the way."

"That's the way to talk!" he said with relief. "She'll go for you. I was hoping that you'd take her in hand."

He was cheered, and she pretended to be, and when Mrs. Kennedy came downstairs they were drinking cocktails with some effect of gaiety. "Beautiful!" said Mr. Kennedy, rising. "You're a picture, my dear. That color becomes you."

"I'd planned to wear the emeralds, Robert, but I took them off again. They were so heavy."

Later, watching how skillfully her mother gave the impression

95

of eating without eating, Dolores said to Mr. Florian, "What's the name of the ballet where the clown breaks out of the box? You know. He tries to batter the walls or to scale them, and he flutters and leaps——"

"Petrouchka," said Mr. Florian. "What made you think of him?"

"I don't know," she said, "but when I saw the dance as a child, I was always so glad when he finally broke the wall and jumped through. Even though he died later, because of it, I was glad. But now I think——"

"Yes?" He leaned forward, encouraging her, and, though she saw now where the train of thought was leading her and would have preferred not to voice it, she was obliged to continue.

"Now I think that, when bad fortune overtook him, he must have looked back at the box, not as a prison, but as a place where he might have been happy if he had stayed." I am luckier than Petrouchka, she thought. I could not break out, and I am glad I failed. How wonderful that no one—not the police nor Richard nor my parents—knows how close I came.

Paul Winkworth was a clever prosecuting attorney, and Paul thought they had a case against Harper.

"What more do you want?" he asked Inspector Davis. "He's lied about being at home that night, we have proof that he wasn't there. He burned an overcoat that he said he didn't have, and you can bet your bottom dollar it was bloodstained. The watchman at Stone Oaks damned near identified him, and now Gus Linke has identified him——"

"Don't count on Linke, Paul. A good lawyer would make mincemeat of him. The first time I talked with him, Linke couldn't describe Miss Waring's escort at all."

"Well, he's had time to think since then."

"He's had time to read the newspapers since then. I tell you, he'll go to pieces on the stand. His identification isn't worth a nickel. He thinks he's telling the truth, but actually he's drunk with the glory of being important."

The lawyer threw up his hands. "Well, we have enough without him. Granahan's a steady man."

"Too steady to say more than that Harper could have been the man he saw. The defense will produce several other fellows the same size and shape as Harper, and Granahan will have to admit it could have been any of 'em." He leaned back in his chair. "You asked me what I'm waiting for. Motive. He doesn't seem to me to be the sort to go off his head and kill from impulse. He'd have to have a reason, and we've found no sign of one yet."

"Her pregnancy was the reason! She'd been playing around with another man, Harper finds it out, they quarrel, and he kills her." He looked at the inspector defiantly. "What's wrong with that?"

"Everything. First, we've found no trace of the other man, if there was one. He didn't telephone her at her apartment, and he never went there. Her sister vouches for that, and, believe me, if the sister could produce that man, she would. She's devoted to Harper."

"Joan Waring? She's not telling all she knows. Maybe she's been in cahoots with Harper on this whole deal."

"No. She was fond of her sister."

Paul looked sullen. "You're heading for a nice impasse. It's going to turn out that Harper didn't do it and nobody else did it either. Only how are you going to explain away the body?"

"I'll tell you something, Paul. If Linke hadn't crossed us up by deciding the man with Felicia in his restaurant was Harper, we'd be in better shape. The only hint we've had of the other man and it blows up in our faces! Now we have to be patient and wait. We're checking all the doctors in three states to see if Felicia went to any of them, for prenatal advice or for an abortion, whichever it was. So far, nothing. We're plowing back through all the people who were ever employed in Felicia's office to see if we can find a trace of any other man but Harper who might have been deeply involved with her. Nothing there yet, either. We're waiting for reports to come in from marriage-license bureaus everywhere, to see if Felicia was secretly married to somebody, Harper or otherwise. It all takes time." He sighed. "And after we get the answers to those questions, there'll still be a hell of a lot of things we'll need to know."

The prosecutor reached for his hat. "I know you're thorough,

Walt, and I respect you for it. But I'm under a good bit of pressure on this thing. The newspapers——"

"Have tried Harper and found him guilty," said the inspector. "It's easy for them. They're not hampered by facts."

"You find me a motive for Harper," said Paul grimly, "and I'll guarantee that the rest of the facts will fall in line."

He walked out with the firm step of a man who knew where he was going, and the inspector felt a fleeting envy. How much more pleasant it was to be a hunter, enjoying a springing ride and an easy kill, than to be one of the sweating, laboring hounds that had to chase the fox to bay and hold him there until the pink coats arrived. And what hell there would be to pay if the leader of the pack were proved to have taken the wrong trail, belled on the wrong scent! Yet the inspector was not at all sure that Harper was the right quarry. What Paul wanted was a target for legal pyrotechnics; what the inspector wanted was to catch a murderer. There was a difference.

As it often did, when he thought of the Waring case the name of Dolores Kennedy floated into his mind. Dolores had lived at Stone Oaks, where Felicia had gone but once in her life. Dolores had been followed by a strange man, for no reason that she knew of, and in Felicia's purse there had been a scrap of paper on which Dolores had written. Yet Harper had never met Dolores. (Q. Do you know a girl named Dolores Kennedy? A. No, I don't think so. Does she live here? Q. She goes to school here. Her father is Robert Kennedy. A. Is that the insurance Kennedy? I believe my father knows him. Q. You yourself have not met Mr. Kennedy? A. No. I've only heard him spoken of. Before he retired, my father was a vice-president of Markham Motors, and I believe he became acquainted with Mr. Kennedy in a business capacity. Q. This is a picture of his daughter. Do you recognize her? A. (*Slowly.*) No. She reminds me of somebody, though. Of somebody in the movies? Q. Think. A. Oh, my God, it's—no, no, I don't know her.) And Felicia had not known Dolores, according to Joan Waring. And Dolores denied knowing Felicia, except for a brief meeting on the train. A regular rat's nest of coincidence, a jumble of effects without causes!

Well, if the prowling man had killed the wrong girl, chances were that he would rectify his mistake. ("If I wait long enough," thought the inspector sardonically, "he'll kill Dolores and then I'll know who killed Felicia. A fine method of detection!") But if Felicia had been the right victim, then Dolores was completely out of it. She had been very ill—confidentially the doctor had told him that they feared for her mind—and now her mother was down with something. If Harper came to trial, they'd never get her into court, her father and a battery of doctors and lawyers would see to that. And there was no real reason why she should come East in poor health when all she could contribute was the time and place of her falling over Felicia's body. A deposition would take care of that.

His disgust with his own powers of reasoning gave him courage to do something he had put off for two days. He put in a telephone call to Kathryn Stone at Stone Oaks. "I have two tickets to this Miller play," he said gruffly. "Do you want to go?"

"I'd love to," said Miss Stone. "What night?"

"Well, tonight."

"Fine. Shall I save you the trip out here by meeting you in town?"

"No, I'll call for you at seven-thirty."

Going down to the garage, he warned himself against elation. Compared to the women he had known—his mother, his wife, their friends, the women brought in by the patrol cars—Miss Stone was as remote as a star. Would she have been just as pleasant to anyone else? Did it just happen that she had a free evening and wanted to see the play? (No, she'd accepted before she knew which evening.) Still, with her it was hard to tell where good manners left off and genuine liking began, so deeply were the manners ingrained.

That was his trouble with the Waring case right there. With Miss Stone and the Kennedys, with young Jordan and Joan Waring and Thomas Harper, the inspector was out of his class. They were glamorous people, assured, well-groomed, poised, polished; and he, as an overgrown country boy with a painfully acquired education and an inquiring mind that took nothing for granted, was impressed by them, charmed out of his rightful wits. He *liked* them, that was

99

the whole damned trouble. But liking or no, if there was a murderer among them, he would ferret him out.

The prosecutor himself brought Celine Zambrocki to the inspector's office. She was a spare dark woman, dressed in a neat black coat, a sensible hat, and black cotton gloves. Her mouth was a thin, straight line and the vigorous wind of early March had not been able to liven the sallowness of her complexion. Paul said, "Miss Zambrocki was maid to the Waring girls. She has something to tell you. Better get Bates in here to take it down."

Miss Zambrocki told a firm, direct story. She had stayed late to serve dinner for the girls one evening last October and had overheard a quarrel between Miss Felicia and Mr. Harper.

"You know how people are with their help," she said. "After a while they don't pay any more attention to them than they do to a piece of furniture. Miss Joan had gone on to a movie with the other members of the party, and I think Miss Felicia had forgotten that I was there."

"Did you live with the Warings?"

"No. I have a room at my aunt's. I work out by the day."

"And how many days a week did you work for the Warings?"

"Six."

"Can you remember the exact date of the evening of the quarrel?"

"Yes. It was October 25."

"Two weeks before the murder," said the prosecutor significantly.

"To your knowledge, had there been any previous quarrel between Miss Waring and Mr. Harper?"

"No. But things weren't the same between them as they had been. He didn't come as often, and sometimes, when he did come, Miss Felicia wouldn't be home and he'd sit and talk to Miss Joan awhile and leave."

"You knew of no reason for any estrangement? Miss Felicia never commented on it?"

"She wouldn't, she wasn't the sort. Close-mouthed, Miss Felicia was, and businesslike. Not giggly and scatterbrained like Miss Joan."

"Get on to the quarrel," said Paul impatiently.

"Well, they were supposed to go on to the show with the others, but Miss Felicia said she had a headache and Mr. Harper said he'd stay with her. She didn't like that. The minute they were alone she said, 'I wish you'd gone with them, Tom, I want to go to bed.' And he said, 'I think it's time we had a talk. After all, I have certain claims on you.' That made her angry. 'If you mean this,' she said, 'you can have it back.'" Miss Zambrocki tapped a black cotton finger on the desk. "That must have been when she took off her engagement ring and threw it at him. I found it under the coffee table the next morning and put it back in her jewel case."

"Did she resume wearing it after that night?"

"No. It stayed in the case. It was there when she was killed."

"What did he say then?"

"He said, 'You're crazy.' And she said, 'If I am, you've driven me to it, with your spying and nagging. Let me alone.' I was in the kitchen washing dishes by that time and the refrigerator was going so I couldn't hear so well. Next thing I knew, she was crying and talking about how jealous he was. 'I can't stand it,' she said. 'It's like being in jail. I'm a free agent, and don't you forget it. You'll never own me.'" She paused dramatically. "And then Mr. Harper said, 'I warn you, Felicia, that you're heading for serious trouble. Stop now or it'll be too late.' The way he said it—well, I hope nobody ever talks to me that way."

"He was angry?"

"Was he! 'I'd like to wring your neck,' he said. And she said she didn't care if he did, she'd be better off dead."

"You gathered that she was reproaching him for something he'd done?"

"Yes. The jealousy and the nagging and spying."

"Spying," said the inspector thoughtfully. "Go on."

"She was at her rope's end then, crying and carrying on. She didn't listen to him any more. She screamed 'Get out! Get out!' and finally he went. 'Don't think you can get away with this,' he said at the door. 'We'll settle this, but not this way.'"

"Did he say those words as you are saying them, Miss Zambrocki? Threateningly?"

Miss Zambrocki shivered. "He certainly did. He sounded as if he'd like to kill her."

"And he left then?"

"Yes."

"And Miss Waring?"

"Went into her bedroom and closed the door. She was still there when I left at ten o'clock."

"Do you read the newspapers, Miss Zambrocki?"

"Yes."

"At the time of Miss Waring's death, were you not questioned by the police concerning anything in Miss Waring's life that might have had a bearing on her death?"

Miss Zambrocki's histrionic glow faded and left her sulky. "Yes."

"Why did you say nothing about this incident at that time?"

"I didn't think it was important. Every couple quarrels once in a while."

"But, according to you, this was more than an ordinary quarrel."

Paul intervened. "At that time, Miss Zambrocki considered herself as part of the family. She had worked for the Warings every day for five years. It was natural that she should be loyal."

The inspector kept his eyes on the maid. "And you no longer feel the same loyalty?"

"Miss Joan discharged me yesterday," said Miss Zambrocki briefly. "Two weeks' pay, as notice. I'm hunting for a job."

"Why did she discharge you?"

"She's letting the apartment go. Just going to take a room somewhere, she says. I said that that was a queer way for a young girl with plenty of money to live, almost improper you might say, and she said that she didn't care how she lived until Felicia's murderer had been caught." Miss Zambrocki shrugged. " 'The police will catch the murderer,' I told her; 'it isn't up to you.' But of course it was just an excuse for getting rid of me. I might have saved my breath."

"Why do you think she wanted to get rid of you?"

"The only thing I can think of is that she didn't want me to see how thick she was with Mr. Harper. It didn't look right, and I said so once."

102

"Are you intimating that Miss Joan is carrying on an affair with Mr. Harper?"

"No, I wouldn't say that." She pursed her lips virtuously. "I don't know."

He sent her out with Bates, who would prepare the typewritten copy of her statement for signature, and turned to Paul. "Not the perfect witness, Miss Zambrocki. Shows signs of bias. Feeling vengeful because she's lost her job."

It was no use. Paul was logical and Paul was sure; and to combat that logic and certainty, the inspector had only a deep, inarticulate feeling that something was still missing, that they were not yet on the right track.

"We've got him," Paul kept saying. "Motive, threats, opportunity, everything. We've got him, Walt."

"But isn't there a chance that——"

The contest was unequal. In the end, with the prosecutor standing at his shoulder, Inspector Davis was forced to give the order that would deliver Thomas Harper into the arms of the law, charged with murder in the first degree.

6

Carcinoma. A pretty word, a poetic word. When the doctors spoke they said "cancer," but when they wrote, it was "carcinoma," and you felt its sleepy inflection trail soundlessly across your larynx. For this word they removed a section of her mother's bladder; and against the repetition of this word there must be a five-year period of watchfulness. For weeks Dolores lived at the hospital. There were nurses right around the clock, but she did not leave the bedside unless her father was there to relieve her. The two of them exchanged bulletins in passing.

"How is she this afternoon?"

"Doing well, the doctor says."

"Never mind the doctor. What do you think?"

"I can't see any change from yesterday."

She lost all track of time. In April—was it in April?—her father's attorney, Mr. Belmont, came to the house to take her sworn statement about the finding of Felicia Waring's body.

"For the Harper trial," he said. "Under the circumstances you won't be expected to attend."

Dictating her carefully deleted account of that long-ago night brought back her uneasiness at not being completely honest. "I'm afraid none of this will be of much help to them," she said.

"It's a shame to have bothered you at all, at a time like this," he said. "This is the last you'll hear of it."

"How long does a trial like this take?"

"Hard to say. One month. Two months. All depends." He folded the paper carefully. "They're barking up the wrong tree, from what your father tells me."

"He doesn't believe that Mr. Harper killed her?"

"No. Says he knows the family."

She remembered that Richard was an orphan, an adopted child, and she spoke without meaning to. "Is that all one has to know about a person? His family?"

Mr. Belmont evinced agitation. "I certainly didn't mean to imply that your father is a snob. He's one of the most democratic men I know."

"Yes," she said quickly. "Oh yes."

"What I believe Mr. Kennedy meant was that certain people simply do not do certain things. For instance, it would be ridiculous for anyone to suspect you of doing anything underhanded."

"I see," she said. "Thank you."

"Now, if I were the police, I'd be looking for a man who makes a business of acquiring young women. I don't know whether he'd be young or middle-aged, but he'd have to be charming, fascinating to women, very attractive"—he cleared his throat—"sexually. That kind of man carries on a whole series of affairs at once, and the trouble he runs into is when he becomes involved with a girl who refuses to be cast off when he's through with her. Miss Waring was persistent and Miss Waring is dead. Moral: Never try to hang on to a man when he doesn't want you to. There's no future in it."

"Even if he didn't want her, I don't see why he would kill her. Why couldn't she be jilted and stay alive?"

"That's anybody's guess. Mine is that he was already married and she was threatening to tell his wife. Kind of thing that happens every day."

"Does it?" she said wonderingly. "I didn't know."

He was angry with himself. "At your age, you shouldn't know," he said, "and I shouldn't be talking to you like this. God forbid that I make a practice of smashing youthful illusions. They break soon enough all by themselves."

It was a disheartening thought, but she had no time to dwell on it. Back and forth to the hospital. Back and forth. There at

105

eight in the morning, home at five in the afternoon when her father took up his post by the bed. Back at seven in the evening to give him a respite, and home at nine, accompanied by Letty. Her father stayed at the hospital all night, sleeping on a cot they had put up for him, and he stubbornly refused her offer to change shifts with him.

"I'm not as tired as all that," he said. "You're safer at home with the doors locked. Does Letty keep them locked? I told her to."

"Yes. Why does she? We never locked them before."

"You looked like her," said her father. "A casual observer on a dark night might have mistaken Felicia for you, or you for Felicia. Except for that damnable accidental resemblance, the whole thing would be over with as far as we're concerned."

"I see," she said slowly. "I was the one to be killed, not Felicia. Felicia died by mistake."

"Perhaps not. Inspector Davis thought it enough of a possibility to warn me about it. As long as you were ill, it was easy to keep an eye on you without saying anything about it. Now that you're ambulant, you'll have to take your own precautions. Don't go anywhere alone after dark. Try to be with a group of people, not with just one other person. Remember that there's a murderer at large who might conceivably be after you."

"Poor lamb," she said, "you're all upset. There isn't a reason in the world for anyone's wanting to kill me."

"A maniac with an ax in his hands doesn't need reasons. Promise."

She wanted to laugh, but his deadly seriousness forbade it. "I promise," she said.

Privately, she was sure that the police were right and that Thomas Harper was the criminal. The important thing, however, was to alleviate her father's worries, and she bowed to Letty's meticulous chaperonage. May came, and the evenings grew longer, but always, as she descended the hospital steps at nine, it was to find the tall, wiry colored woman waiting for her.

Letty's medical vocabulary assumed proportions. "Was it a cerebral hemorrhage? They know yet?"

"They're not sure. They're giving her something to dissolve blood clots. That might do the trick."

"She still in the oxygen tent?"

"Yes, but she may not need it much longer. She knew me today."

"I tell you she's going to get well. She's a fighter, Miz Kennedy is."

Sometimes she was so weary that she clung to Letty's arm as they walked, listening to the soothing, mellow voice making diverting small talk. "That house next door to us going to be vacant, Miss Dolores. Mr. MacDonald told me they're moving to Florida. Seem funny to have new neighbors after this long time."

"Has someone bought the place?"

"Halfway. Some man took an option on it, good for sixty days. Hope he doesn't turn out to have six children, with your mother coming home to get well."

Letty's confidence never faltered, but Letty did not have to sit in the hospital room and watch the disheartening drama of X rays and blood transfusions and the conferences of specialists. Flowers came in baskets and boxes and sheaves, and Dolores and her father sat grim-faced among the blossoms.

"Here's the evening paper, Dad. Why don't you read awhile?"

"Last night she thought I was her brother Winthrop. I couldn't bear to have her die, not knowing me."

"I'll prop it up right here, so you can eat your supper while you——" The black headlines leaped up at her, and she gasped. "Look at this. Thomas Harper's been acquitted."

"Of course he's been acquitted," said her father irritably. "I've been telling you right along he didn't do it."

"I'm sorry for him," she said. "A lot of people will always think that he was guilty anyway."

"Only until the real murderer is caught," he said stubbornly. "I have every confidence——"

"Robert," said a voice from the bed. "Dolores, my dear."

For a moment they stood like waxworks, staring at the clear eyes that smiled at them from the frail face. Then her father reached out an awe-stricken hand. "You *know* me, Celeste?"

Faint as the sound was, it was unmistakably a laugh. "No," said Mrs. Kennedy. "I never saw you before in my life."

"We'll have her home now in a couple of weeks," said the doctor. "Once they begin to make jokes, we try to get them out of here as soon as possible."

June was beautiful that year and its bright flower beds and circling sea gulls bred in Dolores a driving restlessness. With her mother miraculously at home, albeit with nurses in constant attendance, life resumed its usual course and she felt a lack in it. There was not enough for her to do. She welcomed the Island women who came to call bringing their choicest dishes, their most perfect roses, their plumpest strawberries. She weeded vigorously in the garden. She went to teas and summer symphonies and regattas. And she slept very poorly at night. Often she left her bed which, in spite of the cool river air pouring into the room, seemed always hot and uncomfortable, and sat in a chair by the window, watching the moon and the dark tossing trees or the lights in the newly tenanted house next door. A man named James Howell had bought the place, and, since her bedroom window commanded a view of three of his downstairs windows, she came to know a great deal about Mr. Howell. She rebuked herself for being a Peeping Tom, but she continued to haunt her window. For one thing, his behavior was a little strange. For another, he was one of the handsomest men she had ever seen.

"Does Mr. Howell have a job?" she asked her father.

"He's a new associate of the Bates and Belmont Trust Company. Goes to work every day. I see him occasionally, when I go up to talk to Belmont."

"It's queer that a bachelor should want a twelve-room house all to himself. Especially when he's unsociable."

Her father laughed. "You mean because he stays home most of the time? That'll pass. As I understand it, every marriageable girl on the Island is just biding her time, waiting to meet him."

"Where does he come from?"

"Out East somewhere. I've never asked him."

Letty had more definite information, acquired from the Wongs, a Chinese couple that had worked for the MacDonalds and stayed on with the new master. "Mary Wong claims he looks like Clark Gable in the movies, but that don't cut no ice with me. I told her, 'Mary, that Mr. Howell got a high-tempered look about him. You watch out.' "

"Dad said he seemed like a nice man."

"What's a man know about other people? Nothing. Long as a young fellow don't give no bad checks or cut his grandmother's throat, men think he's fine." She chuckled. "He's already got some young woman on the string. I see her over there once or twice, thick as thieves with him. The Wongs ain't going to be working for a bachelor much longer, I bet my bottom dollar."

She said dreamily, "Funny that he's in his thirties and not married."

"No girl with any sense going to marry a man as high-tempered as Mr. Howell."

"But you said he had a girl."

"White trash, probably. Must be, to hang around him like that. Not even fit to talk about, to a girl like you."

Everything she heard, everything she saw intrigued her further. From her window, at nine each night, she saw the Wongs in their white clothes walk across the lawn to the boathouse, their high, chiming voices sounding a vespers to the day. Until then Mr. Howell was an ordinary man, pleasant, appreciative, relaxed; once he was alone, the change came. The smile, the ordinariness vanished, and he moved warily through his house testing the window locks, putting the chain in place on the front door, speaking occasionally to the Doberman pinscher that moved at his heels like a shadow. An unfriendly beast, a house like a fortress, and a man who sat quietly in his chair with his eyes watchful above the edge of his newspaper. (Perhaps he was accustomed to the city, and country life, with its spaces and silences, made him nervous.) Occasionally he played solitaire or wrote letters, and she admired the competent, meticulous movements of his hands. (But what is he waiting for? He is not living, he is merely passing time. What does he want to happen?) Other times, at some odd noise which she did not hear, he snapped the leash on the dog and the two of them went out to the grounds, black shadows melting into blackness.

Infrequently he went out for the evening, and the dog kept up the strange watch by himself. He had been taught to lie in one spot near the front door, and he never left his post. Many nights she watched the lamplight glint on his sleek back, saw that though he rested his head on the floor his eyes remained open, his ears were constantly alert. Late one evening, when Mr. Knox, the Island postmaster, brought a special-delivery letter to the Howell door, she grew so fearful of his safety that she nearly called out to him. At the sound of his car stopping on the road, the dog rose to his feet, bristling but noiseless; and as the strange footsteps came up the walk he bared his teeth and made ready to leap. The front door was chained, but she was in agony while Mr. Knox rang the bell and stood waiting, unconscious of the silent terror on the other side of the door. And after he left, flipping the letter into the mailbox at the gate, she sat back exhausted, and saw the dog lie down again, his head still bent toward the door.

The animal became a sort of obsession with her. She was accustomed to gentler breeds—spaniels, dachshunds, Saint Bernards— and the elegant deadliness of this dog was new to her. He frightened her, yet she was sorry for him somehow. One summer afternoon she caught him peering through the hedge at her and she made timid overtures. "Here, boy. Come on over, boy." But he stood where he was, bright eyes fixed steadily on her, until a shrill whistled summoned him back to the house. Mr. Howell did not want his dog to make friends and she had been rebuffed. I don't care, she told herself, I don't care at all. But she did. Of late she had been picturing Mr. Howell taking her in his arms. It hurt that in reality he would not permit her to as much as pat his dog.

Richard called her immediately when he came home for the summer vacation. "Not much of a vacation for me, I'm afraid," he said easily. "I have to go on to California in ten days. Mother wants to know if you can come over and have dinner with us."

She accepted, nervously, but she need not have worried. Aunt Alice was as cordial and affectionate as if she had seen her only yesterday, and Richard made no reference to her last letter or the long silence it had wrought. Even Mr. Jordan, invalided from a stroke, called out to her from his downstairs bedroom, inquiring about her mother's health. A year ago, an evening like this with the Jordans would have meant a great deal to her. Now it was just a pleasant, neighborly reunion.

When her father called for her—it had been awkward to explain that he was calling for her in the face of Richard's availability as escort, but the Jordans seemed not to notice—she held out her hand to Aunt Alice. "I hope you'll come over to see Mother. She's allowed visitors now."

"Of course I will," said Mrs. Jordan warmly. "I've missed her. I've missed all of you." Her look at Mr. Kennedy held a small defiance. "There's no reason why I shouldn't come."

Dolores had never before seen her father kiss a woman who was not related to him, but he bent now and kissed Mrs. Jordan's cheek exuberantly. "We'll expect you, Alice," he said.

On the way home she said to him, "I didn't know you were still so fond of Aunt Alice."

"She's a wonderful woman. I've always liked her."

"She hasn't been near us in years."

"We saw a great deal of her while you were away at school."

"But never while I was home?"

"Well, it just—worked out that way."

She laughed and slipped her arm through his. "She can come now, any time she wants. I'm not engaged to Richard any longer. I should have told you before."

"We knew," he said surprisingly.

"How?"

"Alice told us." He looked down at her soberly. "The boy was quite broken up about it at the time. Has he gotten over it?"

She felt a stab of conscience. "I think so. I hope so."

Certainly Richard, during his short stay on the Island, gave no indications of grieving. His mind was full of the job that was waiting for him in California, and his enthusiasm included her only indirectly. "You'd love it out there," he said, but what he meant was that he was eager to get to it himself. One of the top executives at Metro was a good friend of Mr. Jordan, and Richard was to be his secretary. "It's a contact job, really. I don't type his letters, I find out what he wants to say and then I dictate it to a girl. And there's a good bit of leg work besides, so I'll meet a lot of interesting people." Once, coming quietly into the living room, she discovered him looking at himself in the mirror, turning his head this way and that, and when he saw her his laughter was embarrassed. "Just wondering how I'd screen," he said. "Don't mind me. I've been bitten by the movie bug."

Perhaps the last hard year had aged her, but he seemed very young to her in many ways. There was no gainsaying his gaiety and charm; they obtained from his very refusal to take anything too seriously. And if there was a hint of self-consciousness to his splendor, the splendor itself could not be denied. For the few people whom he troubled to please, he was the best company in the world. She went everywhere with him and laughed more than she had in months.

Annabelle Adams struck the one sour note of the brief interlude. She followed Dolores to the women's room at the Boat Club one night and offered her a cigarette. "I understand that Richard is going to California," she said. "Are you going with him?"

"No."

"Don't tell me he's going to try to get along without his chief worshiper! Still, I suppose he's looking for the cameras to nourish his ego. He won't need you."

"He isn't going out for a screen test. He's to be Mr. Marlborough's secretary."

Annabelle winked. "Don't worry. The secretary thing'll be the merest steppingstone."

"He'll be happy to know that you have so much confidence in him."

"If you're threatening me with Richard's displeasure, I already have it. I hate him and he knows it."

There had been a day when a conversation like this one would have left Dolores placating and sick, but tonight she felt contemptuous and a little pitying. Annabelle was not a witch with supernatural spiteful powers; she was only a very unattractive girl taking a revenge on the world for her own shortcomings. She said gently, "You hate so many people, Annabelle. You'd be happier if you didn't."

The effect on Annabelle was very strange. She colored uncomfortably and got to her feet. "My happiness is my own affair," she said sharply, "and if you're going to repeat any of this to Richard you might add that I'd like my letters back."

"Evidently there was a time when you didn't dislike him so much."

On the way home in the car, with another couple in the back seat, she said under cover of the music from the radio, "What letters did Annabelle ever write to you?"

"My God, has she had the nerve to mention those? They weren't letters, they were effusions. I threw them away as soon as I'd read them."

"You must tell her so."

"I have. She doesn't believe me. She's determined that I'm cherishing them." He shrugged. "There's nothing I can say to convince her. What do you do in a situation like that?"

"Perhaps she'll forget about it. She's going to Europe this summer."

"That's good news. I'm sorry I won't be here to see her go."

Not until his last evening did he show any open tenderness or regret. They walked in the garden, between the nodding roses and the wide, bland moonflowers, and he said, "I haven't given up hope, Dolores. I wanted you to know that, in case my playing the clown these last few days had deceived you. I love you. I'll always love you." In the moonlight his face looked grave and intent. "Whatever changed you—your illness, the trouble about your mother—will pass. I can afford to wait."

"You mustn't. Please."

What else she might have said or done she never knew. The spotlight in the back yard next door went on, and Mr. Howell came out, slamming his screen door behind him, shouting his dog's name. Richard paid no attention, but she could concentrate on nothing but the deep, calling voice and the great black shadow that lurched interminably back and forth on the other side of the hedge, until Richard finally led the way back into the house and took a defeated and conventional leave of her.

During July and August she made a determined game out of trying to meet the mysterious man next door. Strangely enough, though he was going out more, it was never to her destination. She began to suspect him of avoiding her deliberately, of checking his hostesses' guest lists to make certain of her absence; and, on the occasion of Annabelle's farewell party, she made a test of this, refusing at first and finding that she could attend at the last minute. (Through Letty, who had it from Mary Wong, she had ascertained that Mr. Howell planned to be there.)

Afterward she realized that she should not have left her house in the early dusk while her formal dress could be observed; for as she entered the Adamses' reception hall, Annabelle was just hanging up the telephone receiver. "Gain one and lose another," said Annabelle, advancing. "Mr. Howell can't make it. How lovely you look, Dolores."

This last was not one of Annabelle's customary remarks, and her subsequent behavior was just as surprising. Mannerly and restrained, she moved among her guests without awkwardness or gaucherie, her sharp face tinged with wistfulness. Toward the end of the evening she came to sit beside Dolores. "It was good of you to come," she said. "We're leaving for Italy tomorrow and I don't suppose I'll see you again for a long time."

"You'll have a wonderful time. Six months in Italy!"

Annabelle smiled faintly. "It's a combination of the old-fashioned Wanderjahr and the solution of what to do with a marriageable daughter who doesn't seem to be attracting the carriage trade."

"I don't seem to be attracting it myself," said Dolores hastily. "You may run into me in Rome."

Actually, wild horses could not have dragged her away from the Island. When Uncle Win's pathetic letter came from Florida telling of his desperate illness, she was guiltily relieved that she was forbidden to think of going to him. "But if you won't let him come here, Mother, as he asks——"

"No, he can't come here." The slender fingers turned the gray

114

note paper over and over. "I have loved Winthrop, while he hated me. I visited him when he didn't want me. I've asked him here a hundred times and listened to his jeers at the idea of coming. All that I overlooked, loved him in spite of it. But when he tried to get at me by destroying you, when he made himself so small as to encourage you to go against your own good and the school's regulations, then I swore that I was through with him. I will never see him again as long as I live!"

"You have it wrong, Mother. Whatever he did, he was only trying to——"

"I am sorry I spoke of this to you, dear. You are too young and unsophisticated to judge a man like Winthrop. Such wickedness is not within your experience."

Because she could not bear the idea of the fiery little man quenched by illness, lying helpless a thousand miles from where he wanted to be, she went to her father, who assured her privately that Winthrop would be properly looked after. "Cousin Emily can go down from Charleston," he said. "It'll be an education for her. Even at death's door, Winthrop's impact on puritanism should still be terrific." He winked at her cheerfully. "Go and buy a new dress. It'll take your mother's mind off grieving over Winthrop."

The new dress was made of red chiffon by Dior, much the most impudent and provocative thing she had ever worn. Her mother said it was too old for her, a pronouncement that made her father snort. "Anything as stimulating as that dress," he said, "could hardly be called old. I like vigor in women's furnishings. Want something new in the jewelry line to wear with it, kitten?"

"Heavens, Robert. Wearing jewels with all that red would be taking coals to Newcastle, Dolores knows that much."

"I wouldn't mind meeting this man Dior," said her father. "It must take a great deal of imagination not to leave anything to other people's."

In the red dress she went to the Yacht Club dance with Slim Lansing, and the stag line was electrified. She danced a few steps with a black coat, then with a midnight blue, then with a white mess jacket. The brown blue-eyed faces that looked down at her were varied in detail but seemed somehow to have been stamped from one mold, and she smiled eternally and said "Really" and "Oh, I don't know" while she watched the room over their shoulders. She was occupied thus when, at about ten-thirty, she found herself looking directly into the dark eyes of Mr. Howell.

He stood by the door, magnificent in his black and white, talking to one of the chaperons; and, while she looked, he bowed to his companion and turned back to the door. He was leaving, when he had just arrived!

She murmured an excuse to her startled partner and made her way through the dancers to a side hall that led to the foyer. The hall was mirrored and she saw herself as she ran, a slender black-haired girl with red chiffon billowing about her; and she swirled into the foyer as he turned away from the checking booth, hat in hand. Breathing lightly, she stood directly in his path and held out her hand. "I believe you know my father," she said. "How do you do, Mr. Howell?"

For a second he said nothing, and his eyes had the alert, watchful look that they had when he sat in his own living room. Then, "Miss Kennedy," he said. "How do you do?"

"I'm sorry you're leaving," she said boldly. "It would have been neighborly of you to dance with me."

Reluctantly he gave his hat back to the checking attendant. "I'd like to," he said politely.

He did not offer her his arm. They walked silently toward the music until she said impulsively, "I'd rather sit on the terrace than dance."

"Whatever you like," he said.

He found a place for her on the stone balustrade and held a lighter for her cigarette. His face was imperturbable and a demon drove her to pique him. "I think," she said, "that you should accept your misfortune with a better grace."

"You're much too pretty to be considered a misfortune."

"Still, you didn't want to meet me."

His voice came like a sigh. "No, I didn't want to meet you."

She leaned forward into the light, so that he might appreciate the creaminess of her shoulders as they rose from the red bodice, put a pseudo-tender hand on his arm. "It won't be so bad. I'll let you go as soon as I've finished this cigarette."

"The harm's done," he said. "I don't want to go now."

She laughed up at the watchful face in the shadows. "Then please be a little happier about it."

"I'm not a happy man." The bluntness of this shook her and she was silent. He said somberly, "I don't like your hair that way. Slicked up like that. I like it soft and loose around your face, the way you usually wear it."

"Oh dear," she said with mock concern. "And I suppose you don't like the dress either."

"Not particularly. It's all right, but you don't need that kind of dress. Some girls do, but you don't."

"I like the color. It's—gay."

"Is it?" He flipped his cigarette away and watched the spark until it quenched itself in the water below. "It makes me think of a business term. 'In the red.' That's far from being a gay expression."

She slid off the stone and stood. "I'm ready to dance now," she said.

"Sit down," he said softly.

"I'm sorry. I'd rather——"

"Sit down, Dolores."

He did not touch her. He did not have to. There was an authority about him that weakened her knees, and she sank back to her place. She tried to cover her confusion with laughter. "It seems strange for you to call me by my first name somehow."

"You must call me James," he said gravely. "We might as well set about getting used to each other."

They sat for ten minutes, saying little, and yet when Slim came to lead her away she was almost glad. Until she was back in the safety of the ballroom. There, contrarily, all she could think about was the dark terrace and the exciting and magnetic man she had left.

Encouragingly, she ran into him everywhere. At the Island tennis courts on Sunday afternoons. On horseback on the River Road on

117

Saturday mornings. Across any dinner table to which she was bid. In the early months of their acquaintance he appeared to want to be where she was and then simply to stand and watch her, and this she would not permit. Like a naughty child who demands more than its share of attention, she flung herself against the barrier of his reserve, flirting immoderately with him, forcing him to come closer and laughing at him when he came. With other people she was the shy, reserved girl she had always been, but not with him. She was too much in love to be discreet or cautious. (Compared to what she felt for James, her attachment to Richard had been a mere youthful excitement.)

By October they were together almost constantly, but in several ways it was a strange companionship. He never spoke about himself, she knew nothing about him. "I have no living relatives," he said. Or "It's hard to say where I've come from, I've lived in so many places." Though his dark face lightened whenever she came into a room, he had not once said an affectionate word to her or offered her the mildest of caresses; and she was sure that this was not from lack of inclination but because of the iron restraint that was implicit in all his talk and movement.

Because whatever he did or said mattered so greatly to her, she was often miserable. There were occasions when she asked him to take her somewhere and he would refuse, without explanation. "I won't be home this evening, Dolores." Not "Sorry." Not "Too bad." Just "I won't."

She pouted. "What are you doing tonight that's so important?"

"Nothing much. I have to go into town."

"If you could get back by nine o'clock——"

"I can't. I'm dining out and going on to a show."

She did not dare to say "With whom?" She knew, anyway. It was the Other Girl.

From the night she had introduced herself to him she had no longer watched his windows. One did not spy on one's friends, plain good taste forbade it. She felt ashamed that she had ever been guilty of such a thing, and she smiled to herself when she recalled that she had once thought him dangerous and frightened. (An overwrought imagination plus insomnia could produce sick fancies.) So it was entirely by accident, on a night when she returned late from a party where he had not been, that she caught sight of Letty's "white trash." Leaning angrily on her window sill, she saw how wrong Letty's estimate had been.

The girl was sitting in the big chair where James usually sat, and he had pulled an ottoman up beside her. She was tall and slender with dark hair swept up, and her earrings looked like real diamonds. Pretty, chic, well-cared-for, and, worst of all, very much at home. She laughed and patted his arm, leaned her head briefly on his shoulder, sat close to him while they looked at some papers. James went away and came back with two glasses, sat down again with his back to the windows, and the two of them drank a toast to something. Once the girl nodded her head toward the Kennedys' and asked a question, and James shrugged. As if she could hear them, Dolores knew what had been said. "And this girl next door who's making such a fuss about you. What about her?"

"Nothing at all. She helps to pass the time." A car drove by on the River Road, bringing the Doberman to his feet. (The dog was allowed to be friendly with *that* girl apparently.) And James rose, too, at the sound, and pulled the draperies across the window, shutting Dolores out of their comfortable seclusion.

Until three o'clock she lay awake, straining her ears for some sound of the girl's departing, but she heard nothing at all.

She was not so unsophisticated as to think that James, thirty-five years old and at the peak of his virility, should be a celibate. Nevertheless, there was an embarrassment in knowing that he had a mistress. She conducted herself with more restraint after that, making sure that whatever they did was at his suggestion.

"Is something wrong?" he said. "Are you worried about something?"

"No."

"I'm joining the Hunt Club. They ride every week end till the end of November."

"They're a nice crowd. You'll have fun."

"The hell with them. I want to know if you'll come too."

"If you want me."

She had the satisfaction of knowing that he found the new manner infuriating. On a gray November afternoon, riding home through a light snow, he reached over and pulled her horse to a stop.

"I'm tired of this," he said. "I have to know what's the matter with you."

"Nothing. I'm very well."

"Let's not have girlish evasions. You've changed. Is it because of something you've heard from that Jordan fellow?"

"Richard? How did you know about him?"

He said sneeringly, "How could I help but know? It's the great love story of the Island."

"Whatever you've heard, it's nothing to you."

"Yes, it is. Are you still in love with him?"

She was furious at his hand on the rein, making flight impossible. "No, I'm not," she said loudly. "I'm not in love with anyone."

But both of them knew how untrue that was.

The end of the peculiar courtship came on Thanksgiving Day. He had refused an invitation to dinner, going instead to one of his mysterious engagements in town, but he came to sit by her fire in the evening. From the library came the ecstatic voice of her mother winning at gin rummy against her father, and now and then a log sizzled and broke. Dolores wanted to say, "Now that you've spent the whole day with Her, you needn't feel it your duty to pacify me"; and since she dared not say that, she said nothing.

He pulled a jeweler's box from his pocket. "I've been carrying this around for a day or two," he said. "It's for you if you'll have it."

Incredulously she took the ring in her hand, watching the firelight warm the diamond. "How pretty," she said softly. And waited.

A muscle in his cheek twitched. "I've spoken to your father. He doesn't object."

The curiousness of it made her a little hysterical. "I'm glad he doesn't object," she said, "and I know my mother would be happy to have me living right next door, and I'm twenty-two and it's high time I was thinking of getting married. Beyond all that, it would be nice if you told me that you loved me. I believe it's customary."

"I'm a bit too old for high-school foolishness," he said. "I wouldn't have asked you to marry me if I didn't want you."

That was that, and she had to be content with it.

She worried a little about the other girl (of whose existence she was not supposed to know), but, as the days went by without a single unattentive moment on James's part, she relaxed. Evidently he had broken up the affair, and that was all she could ask for. In the end she said only, "Can't we get rid of your dog?"

"Dex? Why?"

"I don't like him."

He shrugged. "All right. We'll get another."

"A different kind."

"A lap dog's no good to anybody. Still, whatever you say."

It was the one concession she asked. They were married at St. John's on New Year's Day, with organ music humming above them and the winter sun splashing them with patches of color from the stained-glass windows. Laura Derby was her maid of honor, and one of the Florian boys served as best man, since James had said that he had no intimate friends.

7

Either marriage was not what she had thought it or hers was full of unusual contradictions. Sometimes, as when a delegation of men came to ask James to join the Island's polo team, or when she saw women's eyes speculating on the width of his shoulders, she felt a pride of possession and was glad; but at home there were the silences and his eyes watching, watching, until normal conversation became very difficult.

"I've meant to ask you before. What did you do with the dog?"

"I gave him to a kennel."

"Could we get him back?"

"No."

"I'm sorry I asked you to get rid of him. If you liked him——"

"There's nothing I like so well that I can't get along without it."

"Even me?"

He smiled. "You're much prettier than Dex."

She pressed him greedily. "Prettier than any other girl you've known?"

"I think so." He spoke with a reflective detachment, robbing the matter of importance. "Some of them have been rather like you. I seem to prefer one particular type of beauty."

Just once did she mention the Other Girl and that time an injudicious fourth martini gave her courage. She swayed against him in the car on the way home, nuzzling his cheek and giggling foolishly. "Whatever became of the girl that used to come to see you, James?"

"I don't know what you're talking about."

She felt the stiffness of irritation in his shoulder, but she kept on. "Yes, you do. The girl who was at your house so much. What was her name? I've always wondered what her name was."

"Constance Ward. She's gone back East now. She was visiting out here for a while, that's all."

"Ah, but you miss her, don't you? She seemed so fond of you and you seemed so——"

He said angrily, "Leave her out of this. She's none of your affair."

"She's sacred," she crooned. "Mustn't sully her name with my lips. Sacred, sacred, sacred——" For a minute she thought he was going to strike her.

The fierceness with which he repelled any reference to his past kept her from talking, but it could not keep her from wondering. He belonged to the Athletic Club in town, had dinner there several times a month when he had to work on into the evening at the office. Had he never joined clubs in other places? He fitted well into the Island life, had evidently led such a life before. Where were the people with whom he had formerly dined or sailed or ridden? No mail came for him except tax announcements and advertisements. No old friends dropped in from out of town. There was not a scrap of paper in the house to prove that he had ever belonged anywhere else.

"What do you keep in that locked metal box?" she asked.

"Deeds. Insurance policies. That kind of thing."

"Shouldn't I have a key in case something happens to you?"

"I'll have a duplicate made." But he kept forgetting.

Often he talked in his sleep—he was a light and restless sleeper —and she awoke and listened, but the words were always jumbled and incoherent. Eventually, as the tossing and moaning worsened, she had to rouse him.

"Wake up, James. Please. Wake up."

She learned to turn on the reading light over the bed before she did this, to ease the shock of the moment when he did not know where he was, for once he had sat bolt upright and put both hands around her throat. "Oh no, you don't!" he had said loudly. "No, you don't!" Bad as that night was, there was a worse one. She had shaken him awake and he lay looking at her, peering against the light. "Oh, it's you," he said, with insulting surprise.

"Who did you think it was?" she said, and flounced over on her other side.

But there were consolations too. She liked rearranging the house, setting the wedding presents in their useful places, accepting invitations, planning dinners. With her purse tucked firmly beneath her arm, she went buying the necessary things for the household. "You need some new underwear," she told James. "What size do you take?" Stacking fresh white shirts and shorts into his dresser drawer, she had a sense of brisk achievement.

By spring, however, it was becoming increasingly difficult to look on the bright side of things. There evolved a series of quarrels, which forced her into a courageous hardiness she had not possessed before. She held her own, though the ordeal left her exhausted and trembling.

On the occasion of Mr. Jordan's death, James said, "I suppose that Richard will be coming home for the funeral."

"No. He's out on a yacht and they can't get in touch with him in time."

"How do you know that?"

"Aunt Alice told me."

"Or you've been exchanging letters with him!"

"That's not so, James. I didn't even write to him when we were married. I sent the Jordans an invitation and let them tell him."

"Were you *afraid* to tell him?"

"Of course not. But there was no particular reason why I should. We were only—friends."

He smiled, his teeth very white below the black line of clipped mustache. "I know you'd like to have me believe that. It would make things much easier for you if I *did* believe it."

"You must believe it," she said. "I love you, not him."

"Love's a big word," he said. "Most women are too promiscuous

124

with it. Especially your kind of woman. The beautiful spoiled kind."

She wanted to cry, but tears might please him. She said steadily, "The kind with which you've had so much experience."

"I've had some experience with them, yes. It always ends badly."

"With their getting tired of your indifference and your bullying?"

"Not always," he said softly. "Sometimes they die."

She laughed. "But not for love."

He leaned toward her, across the table. "I forbid you to see him ever again. Remember that. I forbid you!"

"I am not accustomed to being spoken to like that," she said with dignity.

Eventually they were reconciled, only to have the most innocent action on her part lead to a small explosion. Affectionately smoothing his coat collar down one morning and tilting his hat back a bit, she said, "I don't like you with your collar turned up and your hat pulled down."

Immediately his face darkened. "Why not? It's a raw day."

"I don't know. Some men look all right that way, but you——"

He was watching her again. "What's different about me?"

"Your disposition," she said gaily, and pushed him toward the door.

In June her father came one afternoon to bring her the news that Alice Jordan, who since her husband's death had closed her house and gone to visit a sister in Charleston, had died of a heart attack there.

"She won't be coming home," said her father. "She's to be buried in Charleston." But the main reason that he had come was to talk about Richard. "He'll be back on the Island, at least long enough to settle the estate. There are things I have to tell you about him, Dolores. Before you were married, you might have resented them. You won't now."

The story was not a nice one, and he was a little ashamed of his part in it. "I did it in self-defense," he said. "After all, he was an adopted child, and a man has a right to know a little about his prospective son-in-law."

He had hired private detectives to unearth Richard's parentage. "They had a tough time doing it, but they came up with the answers. His mother was a night-club entertainer and his father was a good-looking ne'er-do-well who drank himself to death. I'm not one to hold a man's heritage against him, but his was so bad that I told the detectives to keep an eye on him for a while and see how he was behaving himself. With Alice always worried, I knew something must be wrong, and there was. Oh, nothing you could put your finger on. Just a general impression of worthlessness. He ran up tremendous bills that the Jordans had to pay when they couldn't afford it and he knew it. The reason he did poorly at school is that he ran around with an irresponsible, reckless crowd —and, well, before he got so serious about you, there was one girl after another."

"And *after* he got serious about me?" she said.

"I don't know. The detectives weren't on the thing then. All I'm sure of is that a leopard doesn't change his spots. If he chased girls once, he would again. He wasn't the steady kind." He said pleadingly, "He always had money and not all of it came from the Jordans. God knows how he got it."

"Did James ask you to tell me this?"

"No. Good heavens, no. It's just that—well, he'll be here on the Island, and I thought you should know. If he reproaches you or tries to——"

"He was casual enough when he was here before. A little sentimental at the last, but that was all."

"That's because Alice was on our side, and he didn't want to cross her. Foolish as she was about him, she knew he wasn't the man for you. Think of her kindly for that."

"I knew him better than you did. He wasn't as bad as you think."

"It may be," he said apologetically, "that I was never fair to him. Maybe I was jealous because you were so fond of him. I've asked myself that. With most men, I'm inclined to overlook shortcomings, but with Richard I magnified every flaw I found." He wiped his forehead and changed the subject. "Your mother and I have decided to spend July and August in Quebec. Don't suppose we could entice a comparatively new bride to come along with us?"

126

She refused, but she was tempted, especially when James unflatteringly approved her going. What held her back, finally, was her fear that, in a long stay with them, her parents might sense her basic uneasiness about her marriage and be troubled. Perversely, after they were gone, she felt unprotected and alone, and the sight of their closed and shuttered house could make her weep.

Well, she was no longer a flighty girl; she was a young matron and thus committed to some kind of self-discipline and self-possession. When she learned that Richard was back, she did not go with the rest of the Island to offer condolences. And when on a crowded shopping street in the city she caught a glimpse of a slender, smartly dressed girl with a big black dog on leash, she told herself that she had no real reason to believe that the dog was Dex and the girl was Constance Ward.

More and more frequently he called her from the office to say that he had been delayed. "I can't get away. Don't look for me until late."

At first she protested. "This is the night the Florians are coming for bridge. Can't you——?" Or "We were to dine with the Lodges. What will I——?" But answers like this threw him into fits of exasperation. She learned to say, "Yes. I see. All right, then."

On the nights when he did stay home he was restless, prowling through the rooms, keeping one ear bent toward the telephone.

"You're not listening to me, James."

"Well, what is it?" Impatiently. Disinterestedly.

Her great news seemed silly now, but she struggled on. "Mrs. Adams just got back from abroad Monday and she called on me this afternoon to tell me all about Annabelle's wedding to that Italian count. DiSilvio's his name. You probably saw it in the papers. He's coming here with Annabelle for a month's visit."

"That's fine," he said. "I'd like a highball. Tell Mary to bring some bourbon and soda."

"They've gone to the boathouse. It's after nine."

"For God's sake, what do I pay a couple of servants for? Why aren't they here when they're supposed to be?"

"They've always left after the dinner dishes were done." She laughed without mirth. "So we could have our evenings alone. Isn't that funny?"

In the kitchen, setting bottles and glasses on the counter, she heard his voice speaking softly on the library telephone, and bitterness tightened her mouth. How absurd she had been to think that he would be entertained by a description of Annabelle's wedding, presided over by a cardinal; with the news that Annabelle would live in Italy eleven months of the year; by an invitation to the formal reception the Adamses would give to welcome the couple home; by an imitation of Mrs. Adams, tilting her head coyly, saying, " 'Veni, vidi, vici,' I said to Annabelle. The dear man was positively bowled over, right from the first." Thinking of Annabelle's happiness made her own situation seem more unbearable. She walked into the living room and thrust a glass into James's hand. "I'm going to bed," she said uncompromisingly.

He did not have the decency to object. Much later she heard him leaving the house, backing his car quietly out of the drive. It was four in the morning when he returned, and she feigned sleep while he padded about the room undressing, finally easing his weight beside her into the bed.

The ugly little quarrels became a commonplace. About whether the Wongs should move into the extra bedroom or not. (She won there, for she could not have the Wongs in the house to witness her perpetual humiliation.) About whether Uncle Win—miraculously recovered and about to visit friends in town—should be invited out for dinner. (She did not care one way or the other, but she was surprised at his resistance to a man he had never met.) Because she would not stoop to talk about his absences, he gave up finding excuses for them, and this was a kind of improvement. At least she did not have to listen to lies and pretend to believe them. So there were the quarrels, about things that did not matter. And there were the silences between. Sometimes days and days of silence.

Somewhere in the whisperings of older women she had heard consoling things about extramarital love affairs: they always blew over in time; the smart wife waited them out with as good a face as possible. Old Mrs. Denny had gone so far as to say that a man *should* have a mistress, it made him better tempered at home, there was nothing like the consciousness of guilt for turning a man amiable. That was not the case with James. But there must be no gossip, no sly laughter, no sentences beginning, "Hardly six months married and——" When Mrs. Florian remarked that she had seen James dining in town with a young woman—"I've seen her before, but I can't think where"—Dolores said serenely that it must have been Miss Ward, a client of the firm.

Just once, desperately, she tried to mend the estrangement. "I have so much time on my hands," she said. "I've been wondering if a baby——"

His answer had a false and hateful heartiness. "Plenty of time for that." He did not come home until four in the morning that time, either.

The morning newspaper gave the item a small front-page space.

THIEF RANSACKS RIVER ISLAND HOME

Richard Jordan, son of the recently deceased Mrs. Alice Jordan, returned home from Metropolis at midnight to discover that his house had been entered. Police believe that the would-be burglar was frightened away before he could finish his work. Though downstairs rooms were in great disorder, nothing had been taken.

Defiantly she took the path across the fields and through the hedge, walking with a brisk lightheartedness she had not felt for a long time, and Richard opened the door before her foot touched the bottom step.

"At last," he said. "I've been looking for you every day. Come and have breakfast with me."

In a fresh white shirt and summer slacks, he sat across the kitchen table from her, urging her to the major share of the omelet and the last slice of buttered toast. She ate like a thresher and apologized for it.

"You're thinner," he said. "You can stand a square meal or two."

They talked rapidly, about everyone they knew (except James, who was conspicuously not mentioned—at first); and he asked her what she made of the Count DiSilvio.

"I haven't met him yet. I'm waiting until the formal reception tomorrow night."

"I have the distinction of being the only person on the Island who wasn't invited," he said cheerfully. "I'll be interested in hearing your impression of him. Meanwhile I'll sit here and try to imagine what kind of man would marry Annabelle."

"I began to like her just before she went away. She's different." The white honeysuckle, leaning against the old window frame, drenched the air with sweetness, made her close her eyes with nostalgia for summers long ago. "We're all different, I think."

"You are." In the silence he laid his hand palm upward on the table and she put hers into it instinctively, easily. "Why did you marry him, Dolores? You were my girl always."

She withdrew her hand sharply. "If we're going to behave like this, I can't come again."

"We're not behaving objectionably that I can see. After all the years we've known each other, it would be foolish to pretend that we're strangers."

"James wouldn't understand it," she said miserably. "He thinks I'd seize any opportunity to be immoral."

"You?" He rocked with laughter. "He doesn't know you very well, does he? The most proper little soul in ten counties! Most unfair of nature to wrap such a beautiful exterior around such a conventional core, I've always thought that."

She could smile now and take a cigarette. "You make me sound very staid and Victorian."

"I've never seen your husband, you know. He must be an ogre."

"He isn't, you mustn't think that. He's just—well, cross and suspicious at times."

"Aren't we all?" he said lightly. "Want to come and see what the burglar did?"

Gratefully she followed him to the downstairs bedroom where old Mr. Jordan had kept his ancient roll-top desk. "The scene of the crime," he said proudly. "I don't know what he expected to find in the desk, but he concentrated on it. Unfortunately for him, all the valuables are kept in a desk up in my room." He pointed out to her the window that had been forced. "The police tell me it was a one-man job and strictly amateur. Sergeant Holmur thinks I came home before the fellow could get into the other rooms. I can't show you our one clue because the sergeant took it with him. The damnedest, wickedest-looking little knife, foreign made, with a twisted handle. He'd left it right on top of the desk."

The lightness with which he treated the incident seemed to her dangerous. "This is an out-of-the-way corner to stay in alone," she said soberly. "If anything happened to you, it might be weeks before anyone——"

He pushed her out the door, laughing. "Nothing's going to happen to me. I've hunted up one of my old guns and I'm all set. But burglaries are like lightning. They never strike twice in the same place."

They sat in the living room and he talked about his plans for the future. "It might take a year to get the estate settled. Two deaths in a row muddle things rather, and there was more money than you might suspect. I'll take it and settle down in New York and look around for something to do. Remember the little apartment we rented for a month? I'd like to find another place like that one."

"I think I still have the key the caretaker gave me. In all the confusion it was never returned."

"I'm afraid it won't do you any good now. In two years' time they've probably changed the lock."

They laughed, but they were on dangerous ground again and they knew it. They changed the subject in vain; all their topics came back eventually to the word "Remember?" And by the time the name of Winthrop Canby came up, they were tired of dodging and spoke of him at length, with fond interest on Richard's part. He asked a hundred questions and she told him of her uncle's nearly fatal illness and about his proposed visit to Metropolis. "It has something to do with his writing a book, and I'm not quite clear about it. Considering his health, I don't see how he could possibly have produced a book."

"Wrote it while he was flat on his back. Sounds just like him."

131

"He'll call me when he gets into town, and I'm to have lunch with him." She extended the invitation shyly. "Would you like to come along with me to see him?"

"No. He never wanted us both at once. I'll call him and go in alone."

(The clock struck three and she marveled at the swift passing of the day. A line from Dante fumbled to arrange itself properly in her mind. How did it go? "In our book that day we read no more." A queer line to come to her now, out of nowhere and estranged from context.)

When she was leaving, he said, "I can't come to you. I'll have to wait for you to come to me."

She said in a bright company voice, "I'll come. Thank you very much." They did not so much as shake hands, but she knew that his eyes followed her across the sweet, whispering grass until she pushed her way through the overgrown privet and was out of sight.

"In our book that day we read no more." She went directly to her parents' house, unlocking the front door, going softly up the familiar stairs in the dim light that seeped through the shutters. Her books had not been moved. She had intended to transfer them to her own house during the summer and had not. Nagged by the verse, she ran a scanning finger across the bindings, pulled out the *Divine Comedy*. The quotation from Canto V, which dealt with the torments of illicit lovers. The immediate reference was to Francesca da Rimini and her Paolo, wife and younger brother to the man who had slain them. Now, what had a line about star-crossed lovers to do with her, who had been out of love with Richard for a long time and was firmly married to James?

The night of the Adams reception, she and James quarreled in earnest. It began with his announcing that he could stay at the party for only an hour. "I shouldn't go at all, really," he said blandly, "but I know how much it means to you. Naturally, you don't have to leave with me."

Disappointment nearly choked her, stirred her to speak with a silken sarcasm. "I wouldn't dream of staying without you. Let me come to the office and sit there while you work."

His scowl was deep and quick. "That's impossible. I may not be at the office the whole time."

"I'm sure you won't be," she said.

"Stop talking like that," he said angrily. "I have our living to make. I'll thank you to remember that."

"I could remember it better if you'd tell me something about it once in a while," she said. "What do we live on? Do we have just your salary, whatever it is?"

The question caught him off guard and he stumbled into the answer before he thought. "No. I have some investments, and there was an—inheritance."

"From your family?"

The self-betrayal had made him furious. "What does it matter? You're taken care of, aren't you? What are you complaining about?"

"About nothing," she said stiffly, "except, perhaps, your manners."

They dressed in silence, crisscrossing the bedroom as if the other were not there. She arranged her hair in the smooth coiffure he disliked, slipped a black chiffon dress over her head, threw a sequined scarf around her shoulders, and gave her lips a final touch of her reddest salve. He was standing at the highboy mirror winding his watch when she came up behind him. "I'm ready," she said. "Will you fasten this bracelet for me, please?"

Over his shoulder she saw his eyes veer to her reflection and widen. The watch fell from his hands. "My God!" he said softly.

She swooped to recover the watch. "It isn't broken," she said pacifically, holding it out to him. But his hands did not rise from his sides. He stood stock-still and staring, his mouth twisted in an ugly, menacing line, drops of sweat oozing out on his forehead. She put the watch on the dresser top and tried to laugh. "What's the matter? You're acting as if you didn't know me."

"Oh yes," he said gently, "I know you. I've known you for a long time."

Disturbing as his behavior was, she kept her smile resolute. "I'll wait for you downstairs," she said, and escaped from the room. Once downstairs, she blamed herself for being overwrought. Surely no sane person thought of the passage from one room to another of his own house as an escape!

Any movie producer, looking for someone to play the role of an Italian nobleman, would have rejected Count Domenic DiSilvio at a glance. For one thing, he looked and talked like an American, and like an American whose profession might be farming or professional football. His build was stocky, his face thoughtful, and his rare smile pleasing. He had, however, two traits that Americans found extraordinary; these were a deep, innate dignity (not of the titular, but of the self-respecting variety) and his attitude toward his wife (marked by courteous formality and a critical eye).

His effect on Annabelle, the Island noticed at once, had been revolutionary. It was to be expected that she acquire a continental smartness and a cosmopolitan air, but who could have foreseen the new amiability of her disposition and the great correctness of her deportment? Her old acquaintances moved timidly down the reception line toward where she stood, very erect in her white satin, crowned formidably with a diamond tiara; but her face was so serene and her hand so genuinely welcoming that many a woman who had expected to be snubbed hugged her out of sheer relief, and doubts as to the soundness of her husband's title were dispersed once and for all. (Only the most secure can be as forgiving of past slights as all that.)

Dolores was the only one she kissed. "Domenic," she said, "here she is. This is Dolores."

"At last," he said. "We have been wanting to ask you to forgive us for not coming to see you the very day we arrived. Unfortunately there has been too much to see to." She murmured that she had thought of calling on them but feared to intrude, and he looked reproachful. "It is true that we were not receiving callers before this, but my wife's best friend could hardly, under any circumstances, be considered an intruder."

The unexpectedness of being Annabelle's best friend flustered her, and she introduced James hastily. "He has a business appointment," she explained. "He can't stay very long."

"Then I must have an early dance," said Domenic. "The second one? The orchestra is almost ready to begin." His eyes consulted James gravely. "You will not take your wife away before I have a chance to dance with her, Mr. Howell?"

Annabelle added her appeal. "Must you really leave so early? Then, can't Dolores stay on anyway? We'd take very good care of her."

Domenic smiled at this absurdity. "My dear," he said firmly, "Mrs. Howell would not wish to stay without her husband. We must not ask such a thing of her."

It was a memorable party. The dancing pavilion, erected on the lawn, was gay with lights and bunting; there were the river noises and the sailing moon. Bubbles winked in champagne glasses, and voices called and laughter answered. Even James, dancing with her and wishing he were somewhere else, could not dim the pleasure of the occasion, briefly as she was to be a part of it.

Count DiSilvio came to find her, frowning, and took her in his arms as the music began. "Please do not ask me what I think of America," he burst out. "I've answered that question a thousand times. And as to why I speak English so well, no one seems to recall that the last few years we have had as many Americans in Italy as there are Italians. I would have had to be a fool not to learn it."

"I am not a curious person."

"Of course you aren't. You're too well-bred, I saw that at once." He looked down at her with approval. "You must pardon me for making a whipping boy of you, but it is the fault of your countrymen. The way they take it for granted that I am eager to become an American citizen! When an American comes to Italy, we do not expect him to want to become an Italian citizen. Why should it work the other way round?"

She changed the subject to his estates near Florence, and he relaxed perceptibly. "Yes, it is beautiful there, you will see when you and your husband come to visit us. 'Estates' is perhaps too grand a word. They are farms, actually. Because I was not a Fascist, they were taken away from me for a while. But, since I had fought with the Underground, they were restored to me after the war with no difficulty. Now they need a great deal of work. The vineyards alone——"

Going with Annabelle to an upstairs room to get her wrap, she said, "I like your husband very much."

She was unprepared for Annabelle's sudden radiance. "I'm so glad! He's unpretentious, and I worry that people won't appreciate him. I keep wanting to tell them about all the times he outwitted the Black Shirts, about the dangerous spying missions, and the sabotage he carried out. But of course he won't let me, he'd be scandalized." She sighed happily. "He's the bravest, strongest man in the world. Who would have thought that I could be so lucky!"

"I think he feels that he's the lucky one," said Dolores bravely. (It was hard not to envy Annabelle.)

Annabelle laughed. "I haven't let you say a word about your husband. The last time I saw you, you hadn't even met him. Come to lunch tomorrow and tell me how it happened."

"I can't tomorrow."

"Another day, then."

"Yes. I'll call you." She reached hastily for her evening bag and saw the knife. It lay on the bedside table, slim and silver-colored, with a twisted handle. "What's that?" she asked sharply.

"What? Oh." Annabelle picked it up and turned it in her hands. "We bought half a dozen of these in Rome. Pretty, aren't they?" She laid it back in place. "They have so many uses that we've already begun to lose them. It's a toy, an ornament, a letter opener, a fruit knife——"

And a weapon. Primarily it was a weapon, but that most obvious use Annabelle did not mention.

No one who could read the newspapers missed Winthrop Canby's arrival in the gray city that spread itself in three gigantic dimensions on the other side of the river. He telephoned Dolores and told her to come for a three-o'clock luncheon. "The press will be here until then," he said complacently. "After that I shall be unoccupied until five-fifteen, when I am to have cocktails with the mayor. I'm hoping against hope that he's brightened up considerably since I used to go to school with him."

She found him in a ten-room apartment which, he said, had been lent him for a month by a friend of his. "Furniture and all," he said, shuddering. "Fortunately I will be out a good bit. Everything is monogrammed but the armchairs, and the towels have pronouns on them."

He gave her an excellent lunch, taking the whole time. "I hid this cognac from the reporters. It's for the discriminating, not the thirsty. You're pale, it will pick you up." Primarily he was in town to autograph copies of his book about murderers, which he had entitled *Perchance to Dream*. "Though, in all fairness, I can't call it my book. Bolitho and Roughhead and Pearson wrote most of it. All I can claim are the introductions and two essays." He chuckled. "Happily, when the average woman reader—there are no longer any men who read at all—sees a name on a book jacket, she assumes that the book is written by that name, no matter what other credits may be given. Hence I am an author, and neither my old friends nor my old enemies can get enough of me." He related a long list of social engagements with such relish that she broke in with a question about his health, and he snorted. "If the sum I paid for my two operations doesn't entitle me to live until eighty, I'll sue the whole medical profession for obtaining money under false pretenses." He thrust a pudgy finger at her. "You thought I was a goner, didn't you? Own up."

"I'm very glad you weren't."

"You shouldn't be glad. My will leaves everything to you. Surprised, aren't you? Not so glad now?"

"You know I am."

For a moment he seemed embarrassed. "Yes, I know. You're a foolish girl." Then his other resentments occurred to him and he lolled back, pouting like an injured emperor. "And what did you think of your mother's behavior? Wouldn't come near me, sent one of our moth-eaten cousins instead. I had to recover in self-defense!" She said nothing, and he waved an impatient hand at her. "Well, how is she? Your mother."

"She seems well. They've gone to Quebec for the summer."

"I knew that. Think I'd have dared to come here if she'd been home? I'm brave but not foolhardy. Wounded tigresses are best let alone."

He had plans for seeing the Island again—"You can drive me

137

around it some afternoon. I seem to have an obsession to take that high walk by the river once more"—but he tentatively declined her tremulous invitation to dinner. "I might not like your husband," he said, with bruising frankness. "What I'll do is manage to get a peek at him somewhere, and if I think I can stand him I'll call and accept with pleasure." She had to bite her lip to keep from laughing as he meticulously jotted down the name of the law firm and club affiliations of his potential host.

She was sure that she had seen the last of him, but three days later he called her. "Meet me on the point at two, Dolores. I'll take a taxi out." He hung up mysteriously, just as she was about to offer her house as a better meeting place, the day being gray and windy.

The point was at the very end of the Island. One climbed a path up the steep slope between the trees and came out into the open on a high pile of white rocks that extended into the river. As she left the shelter of the trees, she saw him, his black cape blowing in the wind, perched like a big black bird on the farthermost stone. Just behind him curved the arm of the protecting iron railing that had been put up since his day, to keep strollers from falling. But, since automobiles had become common, no one walked here any more. The place belonged to the water and the wind.

He ignored her greeting, let her sink panting to a rock, stood over her portentously. "Well, Dolores, you've been and gone and done it! I've just seen the man who goes by the name of James Howell."

She tried to collect her faculties. "The man who goes by the name of——"

"James Howell, my foot!" he said ecstatically. "He's a fortune-hunting murderer. That's what your precious family's picked out for you. His real name is Thomas Harper, and he was tried for the murder of Felicia Waring and let off for lack of evidence." She could not speak, and his voice crackled louder. "Are you going to faint? Don't faint, for God's sake!"

"No. I won't faint."

"What you have to do is *think*. You're in a dangerous spot, you know. These murdering fellows follow a pattern. Not that we can

138

call him a murderer accurately, since the courts so obligingly let him off."

In her mind's eye she saw a blurred dark face looking out from a frame of newsprint. "You must be mistaken," she said. She rubbed her temples to erase the truth she knew was there. "You can't be right."

"Mistaken! Didn't I come back from Florida to hear that trial? Didn't I sit in that courtroom day after day, staring at him? He's grown a mustache and changed his name—two things that hardly constitute an impenetrable disguise. Incidentally, your father must have had to use his last ounce of influence to keep your name out of that case, considering that you found the body."

"I was ill. I didn't know what was happening. I heard—they said —that she looked like me."

"So Inspector Davis told me. I didn't see the body, of course."

For the first time in two years she thought of the big, kindly man who had sat beside her hospital bed taking notes. "I must write to Inspector Davis," she said. "He'll tell me what to do."

"And what would you tell him? That you've married Thomas Harper? But the courts have pronounced him an innocent man, and an innocent man for all time as far as the Waring murder goes. That Harper is now Howell? He may have changed his name legally, probably did, since he was a lawyer and it would be no trouble. That you have discovered your husband was tried for murder and it frightens you? You'd get very little sympathy from the police for that!"

How odd that she should feel better that there was nothing that could be done. "After all, he is my husband," she said slowly.

"You're a masochist," he jeered. "I believe that you'd enjoy having him kill you." It was beginning to rain, and he threw a fold of his cape round her shoulders. "But he'd be foolish to destroy you without a reason, and that reason will be money. I suppose that, until your father dies, or I do, you'll be safe enough. Well, we can't wait for that. I'll do a little investigating and see if I can find out what he's up to. Meanwhile, you sit tight and play stupid." As she stumbled away from him over the stones, he called after her, cheeringly, "Young Jordan telephoned me yesterday. I'll have him bring you to dinner with me soon. Like old times, eh?"

She smiled and nodded, but that and her walking were the acts of a somnambulist. A wordless urgency drove her. There were things she must do and time was short now. At home, she sat at her desk and pulled out a sheet of note paper. "Dear Miss Stone," she wrote. As she bit the end of the pen, seeking the right words, the scent of danger lay heavy as musk in her nostrils.

8

Four days later Inspector Davis got off the train at the Metropolis terminal and, Gladstone bag in hand, made his way to the information desk.

"Where and when can I get a bus to River Island, miss?"

"In twenty minutes. It stops at our north entrance."

Waiting for the bus in the late-afternoon heat, he debated checking into a hotel first and decided against it. Kathryn Stone had said that this was a mission of life and death and had shown him the letter to prove it.

"See, Walter, she's left out all the punctuation, and she was an honor student in English. The poor child must be frightened out of her wits." He had protested that a shortage of commas was not necessarily a sign of terror, but she would not listen. "I tell you, I know the girl. She wouldn't have written this unless she was desperate."

It appeared, moreover, that Kathryn had had the girl on her conscience ever since she had expelled her ("It was hasty and cruel of me. There were extenuating circumstances and I ignored them.") and that here was a chance to make amends. And so that Kathryn Stone could make those amends, here was Walter Davis, taking what extra vacation days were left him to come on a thousand-mile wild-goose chase, unofficially, and paying his own way, precipitating himself into a tender situation where he would have no authority and where he might awkwardly come face to face with a man he had once tried to convict of murder. If his admiration for Kathryn had not been so great, and had his memory of the Kennedy girl's dark pleading eyes been a shade less acute, he would not have budged a step.

By the time the bus let him out on the River Road, he had prepared the speeches he would make if he ran into James Howell. Disarming speeches, about how the inspector had thought to consult with Mr. Kennedy on a matter of insurance fraud and had found him away from home. "I'm no longer with the police department, you see. Thought there might be more money in running a detective agency of my own." A poor lie, but it would hold for a day or two, which was as long as he would be there. He shoved his suitcase into the long grass by the roadside and walked up to the Howells' front door.

A thin young woman with a haggard face answered his knock. "I would like to see Mrs. Howell, please," he said.

"I am Mrs. Howell."

He cursed himself for being an unobservant fool and hoped that the shock he felt had not registered in his face. "My eyes aren't what they used to be, Mrs. Howell. I'm Inspector Davis. Miss Stone sent me in answer to your letter."

She held the screen open for him, and, when she smiled, she resembled more the gentle, luscious girl he had known; but at best she was a caricature of the beauty she had been, and he felt a paternal anger against the forces that had wrought so great a change. "How wonderful to see you again," she said. And again, as if breathless at a miracle, "How wonderful of you to come."

"Can we talk? Is Mr. Howell home?"

"No. My husband won't be home until very late." She led the way to the living room. "We're alone in the house. It's the Wongs' day off."

"Good. The big white house next door is your father's?"

"Yes. It's closed up now."

"I noticed." It was his custom, when he had to interview someone who was tense, to make small talk until a partial relaxation was reached, but this girl was beyond the help of little maneuvers. He came directly to the point. "What seems to be the trouble, Mrs. Howell?"

She folded her hands—a schoolgirl reciting a lesson. "My uncle thinks that my husband intends to kill me."

"I see. When were you married?"

"The first day of this year." She added, hesitantly, "If we were married."

"You're referring to the change of names? He is legally James Howell. You are legally married to him."

"Thank you. I—had no way of knowing."

"How long has your uncle entertained this suspicion?"

"Since he came to Metropolis a week or so ago and first saw my husband."

"He recognized him as Thomas Harper?"

"Yes. He told me he was convinced that he had killed the Waring girl for her money."

"And that he now intends to kill you for yours."

"Yes. I am not rich, but I will be someday, Uncle Win says."

"Your uncle feels that shortly after you come into your inheritance you will be dead?"

"Yes."

"How does your uncle explain the fact that Thomas Harper didn't *need* money? Didn't need it then, and, as far as I know, doesn't need it now." She was silent, and he smiled encouragingly. "I know Mr. Canby slightly, you see. We were introduced at the time of the Harper trial. I found him to be a man who leaps to risky conclusions and defends them brilliantly. When the evidence hampers him, he simply throws the evidence away." He leaned forward, speaking earnestly. "Believe me, Mrs. Howell, we tried very hard to prove your husband guilty, and we couldn't. He was outside Stone Oaks that night, yes, we had evidence for that; but he was there at the wrong time. We came to the belief that he was the person who was following you, and the Waring girl had been dead for at least an hour by that time."

(He had been wrong to tell her that. She looked frightened.) "Why was he following me? He didn't know me then."

"We don't know. He never admitted that he was following anyone."

She swallowed convulsively. "Was it—his baby she was carrying?" (By God, she was in love with the fellow! Murder didn't disturb her as much as the question of his paternity of another woman's child. And a dead child, and a dead woman, at that.)

"He denied it, and I'm inclined to believe him. For one thing, he didn't know anything about it. They were to be married. Why wouldn't she tell him? But I saw his face when he first heard the autopsy report, and he was knocked right off his feet."

Her eyes were downcast, watching her fingers make pleats in her skirt. "Her death must have been a great tragedy to him," she said softly.

The inspector suppressed a smile. "No, he was shocked more than he was grief-stricken. That was one of the things we had against him. He didn't mourn properly."

(Ah, *that* answer had made a difference! She was able to look at him now.) "Do you still think he killed her?"

"We could not prove he did."

"That's not an answer."

"It's the only one I can make. If he did, his behavior afterward was very, very clever. If another man did it, we found no trace of his existence. Of course, in her business, she met a great many people, and her social life was extensive." He pointed his finger at her. "You say you saw her just one time, and I believe you, but all the loose ends seemed to indicate that there was an overlap between the two of you. She went to Stone Oaks to see someone. You? She had in her purse a paper you had written. Why? You looked alike, and now the man who was enagaged to her has married you. Coincidence?" He leaned back, shaking his head. "No, Mrs. Howell. Not coincidence. You were very ill and your father is most influential. We didn't have the proper chance to push our guesses, and they were guesses. But if we could have found the rest of the paper that went with the piece in Felicia's purse, or if we could have proved any connection between Stone Oaks and Felicia, we'd have had our case."

"You're scolding," she said. "I've done nothing wrong, and I'm forever being scolded."

He smiled. "That wasn't a scolding, it was oratory. Occasionally I am too fond of the sound of my own voice."

The telephone rang, and when she returned from answering it she was on edge again. "That was Uncle Win, wanting me to have dinner with him tonight."

"Will you?"

"I don't know. I told him I'd call him back."

"It would be interesting to hear him enlarge upon this intended murder. I think you should go."

"He won't talk about it tonight. There will be—another guest." Her eyes sought his, fell away. "Richard Jordan."

"That's right, he lives here, too, doesn't he? I'd forgotten." He stood and looked down at her kindly. "You must be frank with me, Mrs. Howell. I don't think you're alarmed for your physical safety. Why did you send to Miss Stone for help?"

"It's my uncle," she said. "I don't know what he's up to. If he's right about James, then I'll have to leave him, of course. But if he's wrong about James, he'll make such a mess of things that I'll have to leave him anyway. I don't want that, and I'm afraid I won't be able to help myself. Whatever Uncle Win wants to do, he does; and whatever he wants other people to do, they seem to do. I thought if someone else were here, someone who'd keep me from doing the reckless things he might insist on my doing——"

"I see," he said.

"No, you don't, quite. I didn't tell Uncle Win, but I must tell you. My marriage hasn't been going too well. There was a girl, a Constance Ward, that James was fond of before and—well—he's living with her. That's why he's never home." She rubbed her eyes with a thin hand. "I've been terribly unhappy. That isn't important, but it's confusing. I haven't any judgment left. Every day, all day, I walk around in little circles, wondering what to do. After I'd sent the letter to Miss Stone, I packed my suitcases to go to my parents in Quebec. And then I thought, 'What if she answers and James reads the letter?' and I unpacked them again."

"You were right," he said. "Going to Quebec wouldn't solve anything. It would simply postpone the solution."

"My uncle will be leaving the early part of next week." Her hands were so light on his arms that he had to look to see if they were really there, white against his coat sleeves. "Could you stay until then? Once he's gone, I'll be able to cope with the rest of it."

"I'll stay for a while. Where?"

"In my father's house? I have a key, and except for not using lights at night, you'd be comfortable there. I'd bring you food, and I could talk every day."

"Your father might not like——"

"He'd be grateful." She smiled, for the second time since his arrival. "I'd better warn you that the Island has had its first burglary. You may have to repel an invasion."

He was interested in that, extracted all the information he could about it, and when she came to Annabelle and the silver-colored knife, he chuckled. "I swear she did it herself. The last time I saw her I thought to myself that all she needed was a knife." He was skeptical about Annabelle's reformation. "If it's genuine, I'll take my hat off to the count. She was one of the most unwholesome people I've ever met."

"I wish you could see her now."

"Maybe I will. Where does she live?"

She took a map from the table drawer. "This shows the whole Island. It was made for the Garden Club Tour last spring, and the houses are marked with the names of the families who are living in them. This is the Adams house, at the far end, on the curve past the point."

"And where's Jordans'?"

"Just across the Island from us. Some of the ground over there is rather marshy, so it's by itself, rather."

He asked permission to keep the map and folded it carefully away. "You'd better be getting ready for dinner. Jordan picking you up?"

"No. I'll drive myself."

"Circumspect of you. Come over tomorrow and tell me what went on."

"I will."

She gave him the key and hurried to gather food for him to take along. Through the twilight they walked out of one house and into the other, where it was almost completely dark. "You can use anything you like," she said. "Have you a flashlight?"

"Yes. And a gun. Let the burglars beware."

146

She led him to a window and pointed through the shutter chinks. "My room's up there. If I should need you in a hurry, how shall I let you know?"

"You and your husband share the same room?"

Through the darkness he could see the whiteness of her neck as her head drooped. "We did until last Monday. I went to my doctor and he suggested that, considering my bad nerves, it would be better not to—that I would rest better if——"

"Where does your husband sleep?"

"Downstairs. That's the window there, toward the front."

"Is the phone here disconnected?"

"No. Shall I call you up if I want you? There's a phone in my bedroom."

"That would be the easiest way. If I answer a ring and it isn't you, I'll pretend to be a butler or something."

Her soft laughter pleased him. "You're so good to do this," she said. "I'll never be able to thank you enough."

Recklessly he stood in the open doorway to watch her run safely home.

There was more light outside than in, and he took his supper out to the screened porch and ate it there, watching the moon come up over the trees and the water. He had found a small percolator in the kitchen, and the smell of the brewing coffee made him feel at home. It turned out to be good coffee, and he drank three cups of it, lying in a leather-covered chaise longue and lighting one cigarette from another so that there would be no match flare. Small chance of anyone being where they could see this side of the house, where there was nothing but garden and river; but he was careful. And he thought that this was not at all a bad way to spend a vacation, here in a luxurious house by himself with the loneliness soothing him as a stroking hand soothes a cat. Like a cat, too, he would sleep by day and walk by night, shunning the light; but this was an old story to a man whose time was made up, not of days and nights, but of shifts that came at varying hours and might extend clear around the clock in case of emergency. For years now he had been able to evoke sleep or dispel it by an act of will.

Lazily he began to turn Dolores Howell's problem over in his mind, viewing it objectively and dispassionately, keeping his personal feelings of pity out of it. Actually what had frightened the girl was not her uncle's irresponsible talk of murder, but the fact that she was losing her husband to another woman. If James Howell had not once been Thomas Harper, she would have had to live through her present ordeal with what dignity she could muster; but his past gave her an excuse to call for help, served as a peg on which to hang her anxiety. What Dolores needed, he felt sure, was a marriage counselor, not a detective. The only aid he could give would be to counteract her uncle's melodramatic influence, to calm, to reassure.

Nevertheless, it was interesting to be in this place where there were gathered so many of the people whom he had interviewed at the time of the Waring murder. The same bunch, mixed up this time in a different kind of trouble. Annabelle Adams, now a countess, who had at one time hated Dolores enough to kill her. Winthrop Canby, who had done his best to lead the girl against the wishes of her family, and who might very well have known Felicia Waring. Richard Jordan, who *had* known Felicia and was still hanging around this other girl in a sort of tame-cat capacity. And, as a wild conjecture based on the similarity between the two girls, he wondered if either Mr. or Mrs. Kennedy had had a part in producing a child who had somehow been given to the Warings. (Still, the resemblance was not that strongly marked, and the Waring girl's birth certificate had seemed bona fide. The inspector reproached himself hastily for trying too hard.)

His thinking about that case had always ended this way, in a confused muddling of Dolores and Felicia together. There must be some connection between them that he had not been able to discover, that Dolores herself did not know; and, granting that, the missing pieces of the puzzle might still be found here on the Island. Nothing could be lost by his trying to find them. It would give him something to do.

It was too dark to wash the dishes. He stacked them in the sink and locked the terrace door again. For ten minutes he stood at the kitchen table, studying the map of the Island by flashlight. Dolores would not be home before eleven at the earliest and he had time for a walk. He reached for his hat, decided against wearing it. A strange man in city clothes walking slyly around the Island might be noticed; a hatless man who kept the middle of the road and whistled was just somebody's guest out for a constitutional. And he must keep to the roads or risk disorientation.

Many of the houses were already dark. Here and there he saw a driveway filled with cars that glittered in the light reflected from cordial windows. Long stretches of the road were lost in the shadows of the trees, and, as he crunched the gravel in passing, an occasional dog aroused to sound a warning to unlistening ears that a strange footstep had sounded in the night. On the Jordan side of the Island the river wind was stronger and he turned up his coat collar against it. The road was rougher here, and from the blackness of the swamp on either side the frogs sang so loudly that the rushing of the river was drowned out. He was relieved when his flashlight picked up the mailbox by the road that said "Frank Jordan" and the driveway just beyond.

He turned off his light and took to the grass, grateful for the lights that had been left on in a house that he knew was empty. He assumed that they were precautionary lights, left to discourage the thief who had tried before. With their help he progressed, stumbling and dodging, to within fifty paces of the house.

The sound that stopped him in his tracks was that of a man clearing his throat. He leaned against a tree trunk and listened. Someone was stirring, but the frogs and the wind confused the inspector's ears. Then, ahead of him, a bit of blackness moved, and he saw a man making for the house, cautiously, stealthily. The inspector waited. He had no wish to catch up with the man. All he wanted was a good look at him.

From the time that elapsed between his first glimpse of the man and his second, he judged that the fellow had circled the house, trying to find a way in. He reappeared, crossing the section of lawn that was brightened by the garage light, bent and running low, and the inspector nodded with satisfaction. The face had been indistinct, but he would know the man again when he met him. Few men moved as well or as strongly as that.

149

And then his ears picked up what the other man must have already heard, and his satisfaction changed to dismay. A car was coming down the road, idling comfortably, and its spotlight played on the roadside. The police, by all that was holy! As they turned into the drive, the inspector flung himself flat on the ground, rolling into the nearest muddy declivity. He heard the troopers talking, listened to their testing of windows and doors, stayed face down in the mud until the last sound of their departing motor had died away. The only care he need exercise from here on was to get home without anyone seeing him. It was a cinch that the other trespasser was a good mile away by now.

But he had been detained longer than he had planned. Hardly had he gained a safe haven in the shrubbery of the Kennedys' front yard when Dolores Howell's car pulled up in her own driveway, and another car stopped in the road. A voice called, "Shall I put that in the garage for you?"

She called back, "No, thank you, Richard. I'll leave it here."

"I'll wait until you're in. Got your latchkey?"

"I have it. Good night."

She went into the house immediately, and the porch light went off. Jordan drove away. The inspector raised his head and saw brightness spring up in the windows of her room. He watched until they darkened again. So much for that. She was safe in bed.

He was about to turn away when something flickered in the periphery of his vision and he leaned forward like a bird dog on point. A man was standing on the Howell front porch. His silhouette was plain against the lighted windows behind him. A big man, waiting, very still. Where had he come from, without a sound? What was he going to do? Fifteen minutes went by. Twenty. The man was still there. The inspector waited.

The ending was anti-climactic. The man raised an arm, threw something out toward the road. Then he set a key in the front-door lock and walked into the house. James Howell had come home.

Much later the inspector went to look for the thing that had been thrown, and he found it. It was a heavy piece of wood, the size and weight of a club.

He said to Dolores the next morning, "Well, what kind of time did you have?"

"A good time. I'm glad I went."

"I saw you come home."

She colored a little. "I thought you might be somewhere around."

"Jordan didn't walk you up to the door. In my day we made quite a point of that. Have the rules changed?"

"No. He wanted to, but I told him it was better not. He—he has an idea he's still in love with me, and it makes things difficult."

"He must be hoping, along with Mr. Canby, for your divorce."

"I don't know what Uncle Win has told him. Something, I'm sure, because he was very solicitous all evening and that's not like him."

"But your uncle didn't mention the matter openly?"

"No. Oh no."

"You're a tough witness," he said. "I have to dig at you. Tell me what went on from beginning to end. Was Mr. Canby in good humor?"

"Very. I've never seen him so jovial." Her attempt at a smile was pathetic. "He's found out about Constance Ward. He says she lives on Oakwood Boulevard, that she rented an apartment there about a month ago."

"Does that coincide with your husband's absences?"

"Yes. He began staying away from home about then." Her face wore a sad puzzlement. "I wonder where she was before and what she did with the dog."

"Dog? What dog?"

It was the first he had heard about Dex. "When I asked James, he said he'd given him to a kennel. But I'm sure I saw her walking him one day. He's a big dog. A lot of places wouldn't allow her to keep him."

"If he's been with her all these months, it should be very easy to trace her."

"Perhaps that's how Uncle Win intends doing it. I don't know. He said he was going to try to strike up an acquaintance with the girl. Nothing like getting right into the enemy camp, he said. I told him I wished he wouldn't, but that won't matter to him."

"When he tells you more, let me know."

"I will." She looked at him shyly. "I feel better today. For the first night in ages I fell asleep the minute I was in bed."

"Your husband came home shortly after you did."

"I didn't hear his car. I'm glad he was early. He has a dreadful cold. This morning he looked ill." (The inspector wished that some woman would speak of *him* someday in that worried, gentle way.) "He can't be comfortable in that room downstairs. The bed's hard and there isn't enough drawer space. I feel guilty about him."

"It's better all around that he should stay where he is for the time being."

He did not explain that. Instead, he described the running man to her—though not as a running man, but as someone whom he had passed on the road—and asked her if she knew him. "I wish you'd seen him better," she said. "I can't think who it might be."

Late the following afternoon she ran in for a moment to tell him that James was worse. He had come home from the office and gone to bed. "I have to stay with him. Do you have enough food for a couple of days? It will be hard for me to get out for a while."

"Don't bother about me. Just let me know the minute he's on his feet again."

He missed her visits, but he was relieved of the risk of coming face to face suddenly with Howell. Daytimes he sat and read, glancing out of the window whenever he heard a car stop next door. Most of the people who called on the Howells he did not know; but he saw Annabelle and recognized her with difficulty. She would never be pretty, but it was wonderful how composure and a smile could improve a face.

The nights were very quiet. Always when he reached the Jordan place the house was lighted but empty, and the grounds deserted. Twice, both times after midnight, he saw Richard's car drive past the Howell house slowly, and the inspector grinned in the darkness. He seemed to be not the only member in the Dolores Howell Protective League.

By Thursday evening, however, the inspector was beginning to feel a little silly. What in the world was he doing here, behaving in this cloak-and-dagger fashion, when he had real work to do back in Philadelphia? The girl must have woven a spell around him to get him to agree to it; and now that he had not seen her in three days the spell was weakening and he was coming to his senses. Defiantly he set out, before it was quite dark, to buy his supper at a hamburger place he had seen in a group of shops over near the bridge. He sat down at the counter and ordered largely.

"Visiting around here?" said the waitress.

"Yes. Going home tomorrow." On the first train out. To say to Kathryn Stone, "I *told* you so."

He would not have noticed the man who had come in for a take-out order if it had not been for his clothes. The topcoat was tailored in a fashion with which the inspector was unfamiliar, and he studied it. Not made in the States or in England. Another part of Europe had produced it and given its wearer none too much room in the shoulder seams. But as the man moved toward the door something glimmered in the inspector's mind; and as he watched him run across the gravel outside and vault into an open car, his head went up like a stallion that smells blood.

"Who was that fellow just went out?" he said to the waitress.

"That was Count DiSilvio," she said proudly. "He married one of the Island girls and he's crazy about American hamburgers. Sometimes he eats twelve a day. Honest."

"I never would have figured him for the nobility. Looks like an ex-athlete."

The waitress said that he was, sort of, and went on to tell him a legend about how the count had killed hundreds of Mussolini's men right under Mussolini's nose; how he had been a saboteur and a spy and had a price on his head. "Guess you learn to move pretty fast when you're in a mess like that," she said.

"Good thing he was on our side," said the inspector dryly.

From sheer boredom, his imagination was getting out of hand. He was beginning to see his running man in every guy who had good shoulders and knew how to walk. Reluctantly he admitted to himself that Annabelle had done a good job of husband-picking. As a man, and without any title at all, the count was impressive.

"But, hell!" the inspector muttered to himself. "If I were twenty years younger, DiSilvio wouldn't have worried me any. I'd have punched his teeth right down his throat!"

He did not ask himself why such a punching would have been necessary. He shoved his hat farther back on his graying hair and strode along wrathfully between the river and the moon. Habit made him start down the road that led past the Jordan house, and he shook himself impatiently. He was through with all that nonsense. All he wanted was a chance to riffle through his suitcase and find the schedule of trains that would take him back where he belonged.

He was walking in the Kennedy garden at midnight when she came to find him, the sheen of her satin negligee marking her against the night. Evidently she had been in bed, for her hair was loose about her shoulders and she held it back against the wind.

"Richard's house has been broken into again," she said. "He just called me."

"Too bad," he said stubbornly. "If he'd stay home a little more, he'd be better off."

She was close beside him now, peering up into his face, and her perfume mingled with the scent of the nicotiana until he could not tell which was which. "Have you been all right?" she said softly. "I've worried about you."

"I can take care of myself. I've been doing it for a long time."

His tone had been sharper than he intended and her cringing away struck him like a blow. "Are you angry with me, Inspector Davis? What have I done?"

He faced her squarely. "Mrs. Howell, I'm going home tomorrow. You don't need me here."

He heard her long, trembling sigh and braced himself for an argument, but all she said was, "I suppose you know best. I'm sorry to have given you so much trouble."

"That's quite all right. I'd be glad to do anything I could for you, but there's nothing for me to do." She did not cry. There was only silence. "How is your husband?" he said politely.

"Not at all well. The doctor thinks he's had a light heart attack

154

along with everything else. Someone has to sit with him all the time, because he's not always himself, and he keeps wanting to get out of bed."

"I've seen you sitting in there, nights."

"Yes. Mary takes over in the daytime. If he's not better to-morrow, we'll get a nurse."

"Well, you'll be fine, then," he said cheerfully.

"Oh yes," she said quickly. "I'll be fine." She held out her soft little hand, and he took it, feeling it small and cold in his palm. "Perhaps I won't see you again, but I'll write to you. I hope you have a nice trip, and thank you."

He felt as guilty as a boy who has been tormenting a butterfly. "Do you have to get right back? Come on the porch and have a cigarette."

"I can't. James might wake, or Richard might call again."

He didn't want to see the last of her. He didn't want her to go. "Did the thieves get anything this time?"

"Just some letters."

"Whose?"

"A lot of people's. Mine among them. That's what he called to tell me."

"It's odd to find a man who saves all his correspondence," he said.

"I didn't know that he did, but I guess he does. As far as I'm concerned it doesn't matter. There was nothing in mine that I'm ashamed of."

"No, there wouldn't be," he said warmly.

They were approaching the space between the two houses, and he stopped, ready for farewells. There were none. Without a word she stood on tiptoe and kissed his cheek. Then she was running away from him toward her porch light, and he saw her pause to wipe both eyes with her hands, childishly, before she went in.

What the hell was so important back in Philadelphia? He could afford to stay one more day.

He looked forward to her coming the next day to pick up her key, pictured her surprised pleasure at finding him still there, but she did not come. At nine in the evening he went to stand outside the window of the downstairs bedroom, careful not to make a sound, for the window was open an inch or two. Howell was propped on one elbow, drinking a glassful of something, and she was moving about the room, tidying it. As she passed the window, he ducked farther back into the shadows. The poor kid looked tired enough without his startling her out of her wits.

As she took the empty glass from her husband, a telephone rang and she went toward the hall. Howell spoke. "If that's for me, I want to take it."

"Oh, James, you shouldn't. Whoever it is can call again tomorrow. Let me tell them that——"

"Don't argue with me! I'm well enough to talk on the phone, for God's sake!"

She came back, stretching the phone toward him as far as the wire would permit. "Here you are," she said, and, picking up the tray, left the room.

The inspector walked softly toward the back of the house. If he could get a word with her at the kitchen door . . . But she was too quick for him. The kitchen was empty, with only the tray and the rinsed glass to show that she had been there. The advantageous moment was not yet, and he slipped inside the garage, whose side door commanded the kitchen windows, to wait.

Howell's car and hers stood there side by side, and he looked at them appreciatively. Nice cars. For want of something better to do, he leaned in their windows and flashed a light on the dashboards. Hers had a low mileage on it and the gas tank was full; Howell's had been used a great deal more and the gas gage registered nearly empty. "Wonder what he keeps in his glove compartment," said the inspector to himself, and walked around to the other side to find out. The glove compartment was locked, but the flashlight picked up a glint of metal from the floor, and he bent to investigate. Almost at once he snapped off his light and stood straight, scarcely breathing. The thing on the floor, shoved almost completely under the seat, was a brand-new, short-handled ax!

But he was allowed no time for thought or amazement. A door slammed—the front screen, by the high, light impact of it—and in four paces he was outside the garage, trampling among the tall hollyhocks to find screening. James Howell, bundled to the eyes in an overcoat and scarf, his hat pulled well down, came walking quickly but uncertainly down the drive. The tilt door of the garage sighed as it swung upward, and the inspector flattened himself frantically against the wall behind him as the headlights of the car backed out, receded, disappeared. Then there was the comfortable darkness again and the murmurous sound of a woman weeping.

She was standing at the junction of the driveway and the River Road, looking after the car, her handkerchief pressed against her mouth. Openly he walked toward her, and she turned her wet face his way. "You stayed," she said simply.

"Yes. What happened?"

"She called. I went upstairs so I couldn't hear what he said. I didn't want to hear. The next thing was the motor starting and I ran down, but——" She hid her face in her hands. "I begged him to stay. He wouldn't listen; I don't think he even heard me."

"Well, he'll be back," he said awkwardly. "He isn't strong enough to get very far."

He was glad to see a flash of spirit in her eyes. "I don't know that I want him to come back," she said. "I've tried, I've hung on, but if he has to get up out of a sickbed to go to her, then there's no use. No use at all."

"I don't want you talking to him any more tonight," he said peremptorily. "You go up to your room and lock the door. I'll be outside keeping an eye on things."

She wiped her eyes and threw back her head. "I'm not afraid of him. I'd like to give him a piece of my mind. For half a cent I'd——"

"Not tonight you wouldn't." He pushed her toward the house. "Do what I told you. There's a lock on your door, isn't there?"

"Yes."

"Then hurry."

He took up a position between the two houses, the brand-new ax shining in his mind.

Two hours later the car returned to the garage, and the inspector was beside it the minute Howell was safely in the house. He ran his flashlight over every inch of the sedan's interior, but there was no ax there. A smear on the front seat cover attracted his attention and he touched it. His finger came away damp and red.

He crept around to the window of the downstairs bedroom again. The lights were on, but there was not a sound of motion. Half an hour he waited before he dared to raise his head cautiously above the level of the sill. Howell lay on the bed, fully dressed except for his hat and overcoat. Sprawled as grotesquely as a marionette that has been thrown into a corner, the lights burning down on him, he slept.

All night long the inspector stood where he was, waiting for Howell to rouse and make a move to go upstairs. He kept his gun ready, for there was only one way to stop a homicidal maniac when he got started. But Howell, though he mumbled in his sleep, did not waken.

9

At daybreak, when he knew the Wongs would soon be in the house, he walked down toward the bridge to get a morning paper. The headlines screamed at him. GIRL KILLED BY AX, Constance Ward Is Victim of Unknown Slayer. There were pictures: of Constance Ward alive, of a body with a sheet thrown over it, of the hacked furniture in the ruined apartment. The inspector walked into the hamburger place and ordered a cup of coffee. He didn't feel like eating.

The burly man behind the counter nodded toward the paper as he set a cup by the inspector's elbow. "Terrible thing," he said. "One of these sex maniacs did it, I'll bet. Pity the police can't keep 'em in jail where they belong."

"There's no mention of rape."

"The police aren't telling all they know. What kind of guy would chop up the furniture after he'd killed somebody? Only somebody who was crazy." He poured hot water into the big coffee urn, looking precariously over his shoulder. "Good thing Mr. Canby discovered the body. The girl was a stranger in town; she might have lain there for days while the killer got away."

"You know Mr. Canby?"

"Not personally, you might say. He belongs to an Island family. His sister still lives here."

"Sounds to me as if he might be mixed up in this some way."

The burly man's expression was one of pity for ignorance. "One of the *Canbys?* I should say not!"

As the inspector walked out, a black car came over the bridge and turned on to the River Road. Two uniformed policemen sat in the front seat, two plain-clothes men in back. The inspector plodded after them. He knew where they were going. Winthrop Canby had told them where to go.

When he came up to the Howell house, he saw that there were two cars in the driveway, one that he did not recognize and the police car with an officer still at the wheel.

"Inspector Davis, Philadelphia," he said to the officer, producing his badge. "Who's in charge here?"

"Inspector O'Brien. He's in the house. Want me to go get him for you?"

"No. I'll wait. Whose car is that?"

"Some doctor's. Seems like the man's sick. Guess he ought to be, after what he's done."

"I saw the papers. I have some information for O'Brien." Recollection came to him. "Is that *Jim* O'Brien?"

"That's it. Know him?"

"He came to Philadelphia on a couple of tough extradition cases a few years ago. Met him there." He felt a little better. O'Brien was a big, quiet fellow, intelligent as hell. He could talk to O'Brien.

There was a flurry at the door, and O'Brien came out alone. "One front and one back," he was saying, "and keep out of sight. No use letting the world know we're here." He walked rapidly toward the police car, apparently ignoring Inspector Davis, but within ten paces of him he smiled. "Well, you're a long way from home," he said.

"I want to come along with you. Can I leave a message for Mrs. Howell first?"

"There's an officer right inside the door. Tell him."

He went up on the porch and talked through the screen. "Tell Mrs. Howell that Inspector Davis said that she was to wire her father to come home right away."

When he climbed into the car, O'Brien was smiling. "That

advice amounts almost to an obstruction of justice, doesn't it?"

Inspector Davis was serious. "They tried Howell in the newspapers once before. No use putting him through that again. If Kennedy'll keep the press quiet until we see what's what——"

"We think we *know* what's what." The driver touched the siren to push the stagnant traffic to one side of the bridge, and O'Brien spoke louder. "It's open-and-shut, Davis. All the evidence is there. The only reason we didn't bring Howell back with us is that he's unconscious and can't be moved."

"What was his motive?"

"We can't be sure until we talk to him. Blackmail, maybe? Threatening to break up his home? Winthrop Canby tells us that the Ward girl was Howell's inamorata, and we've found out for ourselves that he was there all the time. She had no other callers. Not one."

"Canby went to see her."

"For the first time last night. He says she was reluctant to make the appointment, would rather not have seen him, but she finally consented. He had to make a speech at the Art Institute first, so he didn't get there until after eleven. Any other guy but Canby would have gone away again, when nobody answered his ring. But he wouldn't let a little thing like that stop him. He got the caretaker out of bed and demanded to be let into the apartment." O'Brien shrugged. "They'd have told anybody else to go fly a kite, but for him they opened the door. I don't know how he does it."

"He recognized her, of course."

O'Brien's eyebrows went up. "It was Miss Ward, all right. Never been any doubt about that."

Inspector Davis said impatiently, "But she wasn't really Miss Ward. Canby knew that. He's seen her before."

"If he'd seen her before, there's an excuse for him not realizing it. The head was badly battered." He sighed heavily at the recollection. "Who was she?"

"She was Joan Waring. Younger sister to Felicia Waring, the girl we tried Harper for murdering in Philadelphia."

O'Brien leaned forward to tap the driver on the shoulder. "Make it faster," he said.

161

"Joan Waring wasn't a blackmailer, and she wasn't in love with him. When I saw them last, Harper acted as if she were *his* kid sister, and she behaved as if she were. She was the best friend he had at the trial. Why would he kill her?"

"When he's able to answer, we'll ask him," said O'Brien patiently.

Inspector Davis sat in unhappy quiet for half a mile. "The newspapers didn't mention the dog. What did you do with him?"

"Dog?" said O'Brien, as if he were learning a new word.

"The Doberman pinscher named Dex. Did she have him tied up somewhere? Why didn't he make a fuss?"

"There was no dog there."

"She had one. When we get to headquarters, have somebody check with the kennels and the veterinarians. The dog's important. I think Howell gave it to her for her protection."

O'Brien studied him. "Protection against what?"

"The person who really murdered Felicia Waring." He met O'Brien's eyes with effort. "Before I saw that girl's picture in the paper, I was thinking the same way you were. Last night, when I came across the ax in his car, I had him pegged as a guy who had done it before and was about to do it again. I——"

"Dear God," said O'Brien prayerfully, "he had an ax in his car last night, and you still don't think he did it!"

"Look at it this way," said Inspector Davis earnestly. "Harper changes his name to Howell and moves to River Island. Why? Because he suspects someone here of committing the murder of which he was accused. Joan Waring comes on to join him for a while, to help him find her sister's murderer. Maybe Howell doesn't mean to get married, but he does, and Joan has to fade out of the picture for a while, since they can't explain her presence without giving away his identity. Then Joan comes back. Why? Because something must have happened that made the chase hot, brought things to a crucial point where he needed her; or perhaps she came back to hunt on her own and then he was concerned for her safety. And everything goes along all right for them, until Howell gets sick, from the strain, from not sleeping, from all the running around he has to do. Then the killer, who has caught on to their little game by now, sees his chance to do away with one of them and throw the blame on the other. That holds water, doesn't it?"

"So does the other solution hold water, lots of it. You say he had an ax in his car. We didn't know that. We haven't found the weapon yet, and we may never find it. But we know she called him from her apartment last night, and we know he went. He stopped to get gas in the filling station right across the street from her apartment house before he went in. His fingerprints are all over the place, there are bloodstains in his car and on his clothes, he is now in a condition of severe shock, he's been mixed up with a murder before—what more do you want?"

"All I want," said the inspector grimly, "is to find the dog and talk to two men. If nothing comes of that, I'll concede that you're right."

"Fair enough," said O'Brien. "I'll play along. I won't even ask how you happened to pop up at the psychological moment. Or why, after you worked for months to prove Harper guilty, you think now that he was innocent."

"Put it that I'm a personal friend of Mrs. Howell's."

"I see," said Inspector O'Brien. And again, after a pause, "I see."

From headquarters he called Philadelphia and made his presence in Metropolis official, though his old side-kick, Inspector Mac-Pherson, was satirical about it. "You don't have to go West to find trouble, Walt, we have plenty of it here." He saw the police switchboard getting busy on the dog hunt, and he asked O'Brien if it was all right for him to go up and talk to Winthrop Canby.

"Help yourself," said O'Brien, and gave him Canby's address.

The Barstow Arms turned out to be an apartment hotel that overlooked a small park in the heart of the town. The inspector walked in the front door as a group of men with golf bags were leaving for a Saturday-afternoon round, thus gaining admittance to the building without having to announce himself. But he encountered a minor obstacle in the person of a small, middle-aged woman in a maid's uniform, who answered his knock on Canby's door. She looked like a frightened poodle trying its best to be a watchdog.

"Inspector Walter Davis to see Mr. Canby," he said.

"Mr. Canby's at breakfast. I don't know——"

"Ask him."

"Well, he—— Will you wait just inside the door, please? Don't come on in unless I say you may."

He planted himself on the third rubber tile from the sill. "Right here?"

She giggled in spite of herself. "You don't have to be as particular as all that. If it weren't for the way the reporters have acted, I wouldn't have to be so careful. Mr. Canby's been quite upset."

But there was no trouble. Mr. Canby, napkin in hand, came affably to greet his guest. "If you've come to thank me for finally nailing your murderer for you, Inspector, you needn't bother. I was glad to be of assistance." He said to the anxious poodle, "Bring another plate, Minerva. Mr. Davis will have breakfast with me." He watched the little woman go scurrying out the door and smiled. "I suppose it's difficult for parents to choose names for their children that will be suitable when they're grown up. Minerva! And she hasn't a brain in her head."

"The Kennedys chose well enough. Dolores means grief, doesn't it? Sadness. Pain. *Doleur*."

Canby flourished his hand at a chair by the breakfast table. "The dear child certainly seems to attract trouble. Her own fault. She's meek and, contrary to the Bible, the meek do *not* inherit the earth, they simply get pushed around on it. Ah, here's your plate. Pour him some coffee, Minerva, and then go away. Far away."

The little woman smoothed her apron. "I'm supposed to be off at noon today, Mr. Canby, and I have to get this place cleaned up by then."

"That's your own problem, my dear. Right now the inspector and I want to talk without being interrupted by an infernal clatter."

She made a last ineffectual stand. "If the apartment's left dirty, Mr. Canby, it won't be my fault."

"It will most certainly be your fault, and I shall tell the management so." As the outer door closed behind her, he turned to the inspector. "They got him, hey? Arrested him this morning?"

"He was too sick to be moved. They have men there to watch him."

"Well, he won't get away this time, that's the main point. Dolores is well rid of him." He chuckled. "And *that* was the son-in-law that Bob Kennedy, the astute judge of character, picked for himself. Thomas Harper, murderer."

The inspector kept his eyes on his plate. "You recognized the pictures in this morning's paper? You realized who Constance Ward really was?"

"I had a feeling that I knew her," said Canby slowly, "but I couldn't place——"

"She was Joan Waring. I thought you'd remember her from the trial."

"By all that's holy!" said Canby in a hushed voice. "No wonder she seemed familiar when I first saw her. Joan Waring."

"When you first saw her? When was that?"

The little man looked a trifle abashed. "I saw her from a distance as she left her apartment house Thursday afternoon." He sighed. "I suppose I'll have to be honest with you, Inspector. I was playing detective, hanging around the street to catch a glimpse of her. I wanted to see what sort of woman she was before I had my talk with her."

"Did she see you?"

"No, I was careful. Also I was surprised. I had expected to see something flashier, and here was what looked to be a respectable girl. Still, Harper had always gone in for nice girls. My admiration for his taste increased."

"When you called her to make your appointment, you gave your real name?"

"Yes. Oh yes. It didn't seem to mean anything to her. I finally said that I had something to tell her that would be to her advantage, and she agreed to see me."

"Did anyone else know of your appointment with her?"

"My good man, *I* don't know whom she told. Howell, obviously, for one."

"I'm talking about you. Did you tell anyone?"

Canby pushed out his lower lip and frowned. "I had told Dolores that I intended doing such a thing. And, without mentioning names, mind you, I outlined my plans at a couple of dinner tables, just to make interesting conversation. They were very clever plans." He lifted a hand to stave off the inspector's question. "My purpose was to break up my niece's tragic marriage as quickly and easily as possible. Well, I've never known a mistress in all my life who didn't hope that, in time, the man would abandon his wife and marry her. Hopefulness is the occupational disease of mistresses. I planned to tell the Ward girl that Howell's wife was determined to divorce him, that there was no obstacle to the man's being free except his own desires. What I expected to have happen after that was an unholy blowup between Howell and Miss Ward, which would redound to my niece's advantage, no matter how it came out. If Howell agreed to marry Miss Ward, we were rid of him. If he refused, the girl would be angry enough to give us all the evidence we needed to procure the divorce. A simple plan, but an effective one." He took more bacon morosely. "I did not anticipate that she had a deeper connection with him than anyone knew and that he would silence her with an ax."

"What do you believe Joan Waring was to him?"

"It's plain, isn't it? Besides being lovers, they were accomplices. Her testimony had saved him once, and what reward did she get for it? Instead of marrying her, he marries Dolores, stalling Joan off with some excuse or other. Well, eventually she tires of being stalled off, begins demanding her rights, grows a bit threatening, perhaps. Then I come on the scene, a man with something of a reputation as criminologist and a relative of the Kennedys besides. She calls him up and says, 'Mr. Canby is coming here and I'm going to tell him the truth. I'm sick of your promises.' And"— he waved his fork—"Howell can't have that. He acts, and with finality."

"Logically, that's sound. There's one thing you've failed to take into consideration. You didn't know Joan Waring, and so you can't be expected to know that you've drawn her out of character. She was just the kind of girl she appeared to be—open, friendly,

166

honest. Brave, too, from the way she conducted herself at the time of her sister's death." He saw her in his mind as she had shrunk away from his questions about Felicia's morals and the unborn child. "High-principled. Even a bit puritanical."

"My dear fellow, you're quite a poet. No one kills as noble a woman as that. Yet she is dead."

"Yes, she's dead. And I believe that the person who killed her knew exactly who she was."

"Of course he knew," said Canby irritably. "What are you getting at?"

"I'm thinking of loopholes. Who, besides Howell, knew that she was Joan Waring?"

"Not I."

"Then isn't it possible that someone, having heard you mention the girl, went to have a look at her on his own and discovered her identity for himself?"

"That seems to me most far-fetched." He rose abruptly. "I don't like the turn this interview has taken, Inspector Davis. You almost seem to be accusing me of something."

"So far I'm accusing you only of indiscretion."

"So far!" Canby's face was choleric. "It is scarcely becoming for a man who has failed at a task to show his spite against the man who has succeeded, by making accusations of any kind."

The inspector stood up. "Thank you for the breakfast, Mr. Canby. I must be on my way."

"I sincerely hope you won't come back. You will not be welcome."

"I'm sorry," said the inspector, "but, chances are, I'll be back."

He called Dolores from a drugstore phone booth. "Did you wire your father?"

"Yes. They're coming in tonight by plane." She was exhausted; her voice was inflectionless. "What good can they do? What good can anyone do?"

"I'm doing some good," he said. With false cheerfulness he explained the girl's identity to her. "He wasn't in love with her,

Mrs. Howell. And I'm playing a hunch that he didn't kill her, either."

She said tremulously, "There was blood on his clothes. All over them. The police took the suit away with them when they changed shifts."

"Doesn't mean much. He could have got blood on him without killing her. Touching the body, walking around the room——"

"Do you really think so?" He heard the excited intake of her breath. "Really, really, do you?"

"I tell you he's innocent," said the inspector stoutly. "You just go about your business playing nurse and leave the rest to me."

"I will. Oh, I will."

"Does he seem to be any better?"

"The doctor's given him something to make him sleep. There doesn't seem to be any further heart involvement. Just shock and his cold."

"Well, they won't move him until tomorrow, and by that time a lot of things may have happened. Keep your chin up."

"You're wonderful."

He hung up with the wretched feeling that he might have promised more than he could deliver.

O'Brien said, "We haven't found the dog yet. We're still trying. You find out anything?"

He related his interview with Canby. "He was pretty sore when I left."

"I take it he's one of the two men you wanted to see. Who's the other?"

"I'm not sure. I have to go back to the Island and find him. I'll wait, though, until I see the dog."

"That might take all afternoon."

"I'll stick around, if you don't mind."

"I don't mind."

He saw that O'Brien was trying not to laugh, and he said grimly, "What's so funny?"

"I was thinking of the three prize witnesses that are going to prove Howell's innocence. A little elderly man who's hardly strong enough to raise a spoon to his mouth. Another man you don't know and aren't sure you can find. And a dog that can't talk."

"Don't worry about that," said Inspector Davis. "*This* dog will talk."

O'Brien tilted the Venetian blinds a bit more against the sun. "The heat is affecting lots of people," he said.

At three o'clock Joan Waring's lawyer called from New York to say that Joan had left no will that could be found. "I never drew one up for her," he said. "She had quite a bit of money, and perhaps I should have insisted, but she was so young. Who would have thought——?"

By four o'clock Inspector Davis had conned all the afternoon papers and was gratified to find not one reference to James Howell. Newsprint was rampant on the story of the two Waring sisters and the similarity of their deaths, but the murderer was still listed as unknown. There was, however, an alarming sentence in the *Herald's* story: "Thomas Harper, of Philadelphia, was tried for Felicia's murder and acquitted. Police were dumb on the subject of Harper's present whereabouts." He had O'Brien to thank for such a reprieve, but it would be brief. If the *Herald* put a good man on that detail, he'd come up with Howell's name within twenty-four hours.

At five they found a veterinarian who was almost positive that he had the dog called Dex. "Though I'm not sure," he said on the phone. "He's in no condition to answer to anything, and the man who left him forgot to tell me his name."

"Jackson's Pet Hospital, north end of town. Come on," said O'Brien.

The pet hospital was a clean little building of brick and glass block, and Dr. Jackson was a friendly young man in spectacles. "I have him off by himself," he said. "He's pretty sick right now, but he'll pull through. He's a fine dog, in wonderful condition."

The Doberman lay on his side in a big wire cage in a cool room. He did not lift his head, and they stood outside the screening and talked about him, their voices automatically falling to the pitch reserved for invalids.

169

"What's wrong with him?" asked O'Brien.

"He's been cut with something. Has a big gash along the side of one shoulder. Fortunately it wasn't deep enough to get the bone, but I had quite a time stitching him up. There's another cut across the back of his neck, but it's slighter. The man who brought him in said he'd been in an automobile accident."

"Could the injuries have been caused that way?"

"Hard to say. Sure, the cuts could have come from windshield glass, but somehow I'd have expected him to be more bruised and battered. And the accident wasn't near here, or I'd know of it. So why bring him to me? Why not take him to the vet that's closest to hand? The animal needed help badly, he'd lost a lot of blood——"

"You didn't know the man who brought him in?"

"No, he was a stranger to me. Big dark fellow with a mustache. His name's in my file, if you want to see it." He led them into his office and produced a card. "Here it is. Robert Kennedy. Lives on River Island."

"Robert Kennedy, my foot!" said O'Brien, sotto voce.

Inspector Davis took up the cudgels. "Would you say that this dog was vicious?"

"No dog is vicious if he hasn't been mistreated," said Dr. Jackson. "From the way he's behaved, I'd say that Dex—that his name? —was a smart, well-trained dog. You understand, Dobermans aren't all-out friendly, the way some breeds are, but they're not hostile except on command. He didn't snap or snarl while I was working on him, and it must have been fairly painful."

"How did the man get him in here?"

"Carried him in his arms, like a baby. Got all over blood himself. I said to him, 'Which of you two is the patient?' and I half-meant it."

"Was it your impression that it was the man's own dog?"

"It sure was! The way they acted with each other, there was no mistake about that."

"We have reason to believe that the dog's injuries were inflicted with an ax," said Inspector Davis carefully. "Would the injuries warrant such a theory?"

Dr. Jackson was shocked. "I suppose so." His earnest face paled. "You mean to tell me somebody deliberately took an ax to that dog?"

"Inspector O'Brien here thinks the man who brought him in did."

"Well, he didn't!" said the vet indignantly. "Only an insane man'd do a thing like that. And this fellow wasn't insane. He was just a big, brokenhearted guy with a bad cold!"

O'Brien looked satiric. "How could you tell he was brokenhearted?"

"He was crying a little now and then when he thought I wasn't looking," said Dr. Jackson with embarrassment. "It was enough to make anybody cry, to see his dog chopped up like that."

"I think he was crying about something else too," said Inspector Davis. He let his hand fall on the young man's shoulder. "Thanks, Dr. Jackson. Dex couldn't be in better hands."

But Dr. Jackson was not easily soothed. As he let them out the door he was muttering that most people shouldn't own animals and didn't deserve to.

Early as it was, he must stop for rest. He had not slept for thirty hours, and fatigue pressed on him like a thousand-pound weight. He registered for a room at the Hotel Metropole, ate a solitary dinner—O'Brien had gone home for his—and went to bed. All night long the running man ran in his dreams, and he awoke, unrefreshed, to a cloudy Sunday morning with church bells calling over the quiet town.

Because Sunday bus service was erratic, he took a taxi to River Island. There was no use pretending he wasn't nervous. Long shots always made him nervous, and this visit to the Adamses was a long shot indeed. He paid off the driver, standing humbly in the road, turning afterward to size up the Adams house as if it were a fortress.

But he was lucky. As he walked up the long, paved driveway, he saw a tennis court to his left and a man in white ducks bashing a ball against the backstop. (The sweep of a sturdy forearm, the steel singing at the ball's impact, the backward bounce and the man upon it like a cat. Drive, clang, pounce!) There wasn't another soul in sight.

The inspector walked over, stopping considerately where the clay began, and the man caught the ball in his hand and came toward him, smiling. "Did you want to see someone, sir?"

He produced his badge bravely. "Inspector Davis," he said. "Are you Count DiSilvio?"

"In America I am Mr. DiSilvio. You wish to speak to me?"

"Yes. I won't take up much of your time."

DiSilvio laughed. "You may have as much of it as you want. I won't get a tennis partner out of that house for hours yet." He pulled up a lawn chair for the inspector (was it a good sign that he had chosen a location that was screened from the house?) and sat down beside him. "Have I met you before? I thought not. I'm very good at faces."

"I myself am better at bodies. Posture, carriage, movement."

"That's strange," said DiSilvio absently. "You Americans seem to move so little. If the principle of the wheel had not already been discovered, your nation would have invented it. Now what is it you want with me? Have I been parking improperly?"

The inspector took the plunge. "More serious than that. House-breaking."

DiSilvio showed no surprise. He looked down at his tennis shoes thoughtfully. "Isn't it absurd to suppose, Inspector, that a man of my position would stoop to climbing in other people's windows?"

"Not if you had the proper provocation."

"What provocation am I supposed to have had?"

"I don't know. I saw you trying to break into the Jordan house. A night or two later you succeeded. I want to know what you were after and what you got."

The powerful young man sat motionless. "This is too bad," he said finally. "My wife's family will be very unhappy."

"They won't need to know. I am here unofficially. This interview will be entirely confidential."

"Can one be confidential to a police department about one's crimes?"

"You have committed no crime, because Jordan hasn't reported the matter. I heard about it indirectly. Adding that to the evidence of my own eyes——"

DiSilvio lifted his chin and looked impish. "You say you saw me. Well, I saw you too. Several nights. Followed you for miles in the dark. You worried me. I didn't know what you were up to, and I never could run you to ground." He nudged the inspector's ribs, as if they shared a joke. "I planned the job for earlier in the week, but Thursday was the only night you weren't around."

The inspector mustered his dignity. "Let me make myself clear. I am interested in your robbing Richard Jordan only because it may have an effect on a much more serious matter. Murder."

"But I have no intention of killing Jordan," said the count surprisingly. "In Italy, yes, I would have killed him. Blackmail is very unhealthy there."

He felt as if he had put out a saucer of milk for a house cat and drawn a tiger. "Jordan was blackmailing you?"

"Worse. He was attempting to blackmail my wife. She had written him some foolish letters—when she was a mere girl, you understand—and he demanded money for their return. He made the request in a letter which was waiting for her when we arrived. She finally confessed to me what was troubling her, and I was all for going and knocking the fellow down!"

"Why didn't you? Wouldn't your wife——"

DiSilvio stared at him with soft brown eyes. "Let us omit my wife from this discussion, Inspector. I am old-fashioned. I believe that, since the day we were married, my wife's every word and act have been my responsibility. Not hers."

"Ah," said the inspector weakly. "So you didn't go and beat him up?"

"I didn't even have a talk with him. I wanted nothing from him but those letters, and I got them."

"Did your—did anybody know you had done this?"

"No."

"What did you do with the letters?"

"I destroyed them. Unread."

"Without telling anyone?"

"How could I tell anyone? I had been guilty of breaking the law."

Incredulity lingered in the inspector's mind. "Have you saved the letter Jordan wrote, demanding money?"

"No. I can recall parts of it, though. It was all very smooth and subtle, plain without being forthright. He said that he was rather poor these days and he often read her letters over again to cheer himself; that they were very precious to him; and he ended by hoping that he could meet me because we would have so much in common to talk about. Something like that. The scoundrel!"

"Isn't it possible that you misinterpreted the letter? That it really meant what it said? Congratulatory letters are usually a bit effusive."

"Whatever he meant by it," said the count with satisfaction, "he doesn't have his precious letters any more."

"Were they done up in packets? Each correspondent's letters all together?"

"Yes."

"How many packets did you take?"

"Four or five. I was hoping to confuse the police a trifle."

"Do you know whose letters they were?"

"Two were from men. I didn't pay much attention to those. Then there was a big bunch from a girl in California named Paula, and a bigger one from"—he said the words reluctantly—"Dolores Howell. Written when she was Miss Kennedy, of course."

"You destroyed all of these?"

"All but Mrs. Howell's. She's a good friend of ours, and I thought he might be trying the same scheme on her. Once, when I was following you, I almost ran into him, standing near her house. And she's seemed quite unhappy about something——"

The inspector trembled with impatience. "What did you do with Mrs. Howell's letters?"

"It was a devilish problem. I wanted her to know they were safe, but I could hardly send them to her house, where her husband might see them. If her father had been home, I would have sent them to him."

"Well? Well?"

"So I wrapped them up and sent them, special delivery, to her uncle, Winthrop Canby. He's visiting in town."

174

The inspector stood up. "When did you mail them?"

"Friday morning. They may have reached him that afternoon. Certainly by Saturday morning."

"You enclosed no note of explanation?"

"You bet I didn't," said the count happily.

"There was nothing but her letters?"

"Far as I know."

The inspector started down the drive, so lost in meditation that he neither shook hands nor said good-by. The count, a conscientious host, came after him. "Do you have a car waiting for you? There's no other transportation here Sunday mornings. Better let me give you a lift."

He accepted, but only to the other side of the bridge, where he could get a city bus. He was too old a hand to trust plausible young men on such short acquaintance; on the other hand, he needed to get to Winthrop Canby as fast as he could.

10

Minerva held on to the door resolutely. "Mr. Canby is not at home."

"Where's he gone?"

"I don't know."

"When did he leave?"

"Half an hour ago. Maybe a little less."

The inspector pushed by her. "I'll have to talk to you, then. Come on in here and sit down."

She wrung her hands and wailed. "I can't. I have a bathroom to scrub, and Mr. Canby doesn't like to have me let anyone in unless——"

He walked over to the desk, which was littered and heaped with books and papers, and she followed him frantically. "Don't you touch a thing on that desk. It's as much as my job is worth to——" Her small rough hands pulled at him and there were tears in her pale, frightened eyes.

"I'm not going to get you into any trouble. I want you to answer a few questions, that's all."

She sat down, defeated. "Well, if it won't take too long."

"Are you employed by Mr. Canby?"

"No. I work for the management of the building. By the day."

"How much of your time do you spend in this apartment?"

"All day, seven days a week, since Mr. Canby came."

"Usually you divide your time among several apartments?"

"Yes, sir, but Mr. Canby needs so much service that they assigned me here. Of course he pays extra for me."

"Do you like working for him?"

"He's a hard man to work for, but he's generous. I guess I can stand it. At first I thought I couldn't."

He leaned back against the desk. "He's been here almost three weeks, hasn't he? Does he have much company?"

"Hundreds of people," she said wearily. "In and out, back and forth, telephone ringing, get a drink for this one and sandwiches for that one——"

"Do you remember any person who's come oftener than the others?"

"I'm too busy to look at their faces much. I wouldn't know that."

"Can you recall a small dinner party he gave last Wednesday night?"

"I heard him order the dinner sent up from downstairs, that's all. I don't know which waiter came up to serve. I leave at seven o'clock."

"That's late, isn't it?"

"Yes, but I don't have to be back until ten in the morning. He sleeps in."

"You came in at ten this morning?"

"No, I came at nine. You see, he gets up earlier on Sundays, to answer his mail. That's why the desk looks like that. Stuff piles up on it all week and he doesn't look at it. Then Sunday mornings he sets to and gets it all cleaned up."

"I'm especially interested in a special-delivery package that he received Friday afternoon or Saturday morning. Can you tell me anything about that?"

She shook her head. "He gets special-delivery packages every day. And telegrams and air-mail letters and——"

He walked around the desk, his hands in his pockets. "What was he doing when you came in this morning?"

"He was sitting there, writing."

"Writing a letter?" (He saw Dolores's letters now. They were

177

no longer tied together. Spilling from a brown-paper wrapping, they covered a fourth of the desk's surface.)

"Not exactly." Her face was tight with concentration. "I think he was copying something." She beamed proudly at this feat of memory. "When I went to take his coffee cup away—it was right on the desk beside him—he had a paper with writing on it in front of him, and he was looking at it and then writing on another piece of paper. That was kind of funny, because he usually did all his writing on the typewriter."

"Did you make a remark to him of any kind?"

"No. The paper had blue lines on it. Like we used to have at school. I almost said, 'That's queer paper for you to be writing on,' but I kept quiet."

His feet almost left the floor. "School? Lined paper? Was it like a composition? A theme? The sort of thing you write for your high-school English teacher?"

"Exactly like that. There was even writing up in the corner, where we used to put our name and grade and——"

"Did you see the name?" he said fiercely. "Would you recognize the paper?"

"I think I could. Part of it was torn off at the bottom."

"The paper he was copying had a piece torn off at the bottom. Do I have that straight?"

"Yes. And another funny thing——"

He leaped at the desk, plunging his hands into the papers. "Where is it? What did he do with it?"

She ran to stop him. "You're messing it up! He'll know you've done it and that I let you. You mustn't!"

"I'll take the blame for it." But there was no such paper in the desk nor in its drawers, unless in the one that was locked and that he could not open without legal authority. "Could he have taken it with him, Minerva?"

"I don't know. He took the copy with him." She giggled a little. "That was the other funny thing. When he got through writing, he tore a piece of the paper off, just like the other. Then he folded it up and put it in his pocket. Imagine writing something, just to tear it up!"

"He left right after that?"

"Yes. He put on his coat and hat and said, 'If George calls, tell him I'm on my way to him,' and walked out."

"You're sure he said George?"

"Well, it *sounded* like George."

He reached for the telephone and asked police headquarters if they could locate Inspector O'Brien and have him and a police car in front of the Barstow Arms in twenty minutes. "Tell O'Brien if he's much later than that, he'll be bringing another body back with him." As he hung up, Minerva's gasp reminded him that she was still there. "Get your things," he said to her.

She backed away from him. "I'm not going anywhere."

"Yes, you're going home. Hurry."

"Why? Why must I?"

"Because it's not safe for you to stay here." He added, less brusquely, "It'll be safe again tomorrow."

Fright had paralyzed her. All she could do was make a whimpering noise, and he had to put her coat on her as if she were a rag doll.

From the foyer he called Dolores, keeping an eye on the curb beyond the glass for the police car.

"Your father and mother came home?"

"Yes. They're here with me now."

Her voice was happy, and he felt sorry for her. Before nightfall she might be sad again and because of what he had to do. "Are the policemen still there?"

"Yes. James is much better, but they haven't said any more about taking him away."

"That's a good sign," he said. "May I talk to your father for a minute?"

Mr. Kennedy came on at once. "I've been waiting for you to call, Inspector. I feel somewhat responsible for all this. You see, I knew who James was from the first."

"I imagined that you'd investigate a man who was to become your son-in-law."

"I didn't have to investigate him. I knew him. Oh, I hadn't seen him for years—not since he was a little boy—but I wrote to him during the trial, expressing my confidence in him and so on, and that renewed the acquaintance. The next thing, he asked me if I could get him a job out here, and I did. It was his idea that the murderer had something to do with the Island, and that he could catch him. Well, I was all for that. I can see now that it was too dangerous a game, and I shouldn't have let him play it. The mess he's in is partly my fault."

"Maybe we can pull him out. I'll know shortly."

"We're saving your suitcase for you. When will you be out?"

"After a while," said the inspector soberly. "I have some things to do first."

"Come to dinner with my wife and me tonight. I have to have a chance to thank you properly."

"No need to thank me." He hurried on, avoiding the issue of the dinner invitation. "Are they allowing your daughter to come and go as she pleases?"

"I don't know. She hasn't tried to go anywhere. Seems perfectly happy where she is."

"She mustn't leave the house until I say she may. Will you see to that? No matter what the emergency or at whose request, she must not leave the house!"

"All right. I'll see to it."

The police car was pulling up to the curb. He walked out and said to the driver, "River Island. As fast as you can."

O'Brien was not a noisy man. He sat in his corner of the back seat and watched Inspector Davis scowling for five miles. Then he said casually, "What's this about bringing a body back with us?"

"Canby's got a dangerous piece of paper on him, one of the clues we hunted for far and wide in the Felicia Waring murder. If nobody else kills him for it, I'm willing to, in case he won't give it up peaceably."

"We're going to the Island to find Canby?"

"Yes. I think he's visiting a man named Jordan." His temper

180

was mounting, driven by anxiety and a sense of being unequal to the occasion, and his voice exploded into irritability. "Hell, I don't know that he's at Jordan's. The maid said he was going to see a 'George,' and I took a chance."

"Canby and Jordan are friends?"

"Yes. Jordan was engaged to Canby's niece once."

"What happened to break it up?"

"I don't know." He looked at O'Brien angrily. "I don't know a damned thing about anything. Except that Canby has a paper I want, and its possession makes him an accessory after the fact. If not something worse."

"Do we tackle him in front of Jordan? Or do we just ask him to come along back with us?"

With the prospect of action his self-possession returned. "I'd like to try to surprise him first. Leave the car somewhere, walk quietly up to the house, see what's going on between those two. If that doesn't get us anything, we'll go in and get him."

"Suits me," said O'Brien mildly.

The inspector leaned forward and spoke to the plain-clothes man who was driving. "Pick a spot anywhere along here and nose into the trees. Watch out for mud."

They got out quickly, dispersing to the different routes he had indicated for them: the plain-clothes man to come up at the far end of the house; O'Brien at the garage side; himself directly at the back. Trees covered all those areas to within a few feet of the foundations. They would have protection all the way.

Inspector Davis, knowing the terrain, was the first to reach the house. The living room turned a corner, and its rear window was before him and open. For five minutes he crouched, and heard no sound but the crackling of logs in the fireplace. Then, turning his head, he saw O'Brien beckoning from the corner of the garage and went to him.

"Nobody's home," he said disgustedly.

"That's what I thought. There's no car in the garage. But it hasn't been gone long."

"How do you know?"

181

"The drive's soft under the gravel. The tire tracks fill up with water as soon as they're made, and there are some that've just begun to fill."

They stood and studied the driveway and the plain-clothes man joined them. "Found something," he said.

It was a gray suède glove, clean and fresh, with a few bits of gravel sticking to it. "Where?" said O'Brien, taking it.

"At the edge of the drive over there. It's a man's glove, isn't it? Pretty small, though."

O'Brien's voice showed a trace of excitement. "It's Canby's glove! He was wearing a pair like this the night he reported the murder. They're unusual for a man, and I noticed them. He's been here all right."

Inspector Davis looked moodily at the woods. "May still be here. It's like looking for a needle in a haystack."

"He doesn't drive. And he isn't built for walking. I think he's in somebody's car. Joe, you stay here and keep an eye open for him. Davis and I'll drive around the Island and see what we can see."

"If he comes back here, shall I hold him?"

"Yes. We won't be long."

The rain began lightly as they reached the police car. "You drive," said O'Brien. "I'll watch on this side."

"Jordan's car is a Chevrolet convertible, dark green, this year's model."

O'Brien nodded, keeping his eyes on the road. No sign of such a car anywhere, or of a plump, small man with one gray glove. Cars in the Kennedy drive, but not the right one. The doctor's car at the Howells'. They roared past the shops by the bridge and kept on.

"What's down this way?" said O'Brien.

"People named Adams live past the curve at the end of the Island. Jordan knows them." He turned on the windshield wipers. "I was certain, from what the maid said, that the two of them had an appointment. But Canby could have found Jordan not at home and told his cab to take him right back to town."

O'Brien touched his arm. "Look there. Is that the car?"

The inspector came down hard on the brakes. A little road idled off to the right, almost choked with undergrowth, and the Chevrolet sat there, nearly hidden. "That's it."

O'Brien jumped out before the wheels stopped turning and was back in a minute with his report. "Nobody's in it. They've left the windows open too. Where in hell would they go in this rain? Is there a house around?"

He took out his rumpled map. "No. The Adamses are half a mile farther down. This is the Point. 'Wonderful view of the river from here,' it says."

They looked up at the steep, rocky incline, with the pines huddled together against the wind.

"Well, let's go up and see," said O'Brien. "If they're looking at the river in this rain, they ought to have their heads examined."

"One thing, the wind's *from* the river. They won't hear us coming."

"What could they do about it if they *did* hear us?" asked O'Brien simply.

When Winthrop Canby paid off his taxi in front of Richard's house, he had already begun to act the role he had set for himself as the artless, unsuspicious older friend. The heaviness of the clouds bothered him. Yesterday, when he had invited Richard to go for a walk on the Point—"I *have* to go there once more before I die, God knows why"—he had had no ulterior motive. But things had changed since then, and Richard must not know that. Until later.

Richard's gladness at seeing him was a little depressing too. Such a handsome young man. A shame to think he had no future. No future at all.

"I thought you might not come, Mr. Canby. Weather looks threatening. I've built a fire in case you decide against the walk."

For a moment he was tempted. After all, he wasn't so young as he used to be. "It wasn't *just* the walk. I wanted to have a private chat with you."

Richard laughed. "Then this isn't the place for it. People drop in here any time. Older women, mostly, to see if I'm making out

183

all right." He winked. "Might meet some of your childhood sweethearts if you stay awhile."

"I have no wish to see the elegantly corseted tombs wherein dead beauty lies."

"Then we'll have one drink in front of the fire and go for your walk."

"Nothing for me, thanks. You have one."

He took off his gloves and hat and scarf, but he kept his topcoat on, loosening it as the warmth of the fire comforted his arthritic legs. He said, "Has Inspector Davis been to see you?"

"The police? No. I haven't set eyes on them since my thwarted burglary."

"You know the man I mean? Inspector Davis of the Philadelphia Police Department."

"The one that—— What's he doing here?"

"Perhaps he's come to take Harper back with him."

"Of course. That must be it."

Winthrop Canby stared at the fire. "Had you met Joan Waring back East?"

"No."

"When I spoke of a Constance Ward, you had no idea that she was really Joan Waring?"

"I didn't realize it till I read it in the paper. Did you?"

"No. Davis thinks I should have. He came to see me yesterday, wanting to know to whom I had spoken about the girl. I didn't tell him so, but it was only to you and Dolores."

"Oh?" said Richard politely.

"Can you recall repeating my conversation to anyone?"

"I never gave it a second thought." He sipped his drink reflectively. "What difference does any of this make? They've got Harper, haven't they?"

"Yes, they've got him. I don't know how Dolores is taking it."

"I've been wondering. Better to let her alone until all this has blown over, don't you think?"

"I suppose." He liked to be standing when a taller man was sitting. It gave him a sense of power. He grew bolder. "Do you still intend to marry her, Richard?"

184

"If she'll have me. I've been proposing to her off and on for the past four years. The habit's too strong to break."

"When you came home that summer, before you went to California, why didn't you marry her then?"

"She'd been ill, and—well—the way she acted made me a little sore. If she could be so damned indifferent, so could I be."

"I thought it might have been because of your mother."

Richard's head came up. "My mother? What would she have to do with it?"

"Mothers usually object to their son's marrying. That's all I meant. Don't look so alarmed. You were always my candidate, you know."

"I know," he said gratefully. "You did your damnedest. Shame you didn't succeed."

"In the long run I'll succeed. Dolores is to be my heir, and you will be married to Dolores."

"I hope you're right about the second part of that."

Mr. Canby raised his eyebrows. "And you don't care about the first part? You're a most improvident young man."

A few drops of rain spattered against the windows, and Richard saw them. "There goes our walk. We'll have to stay here."

"A little rain doesn't bother me." He looked pathetic. "My life is nearly over. I may never see the Point again."

Richard jumped up. "I can stand it, if you can."

As he got into the car, Winthrop Canby felt his first terror at what he was about to do. The gun in his coat pocket pressed reassuringly against his side, but it might not serve his purpose well enough. There was the difference in age and strength; and he had been fond of this young man; he might weaken at the last moment in spite of himself. Best to leave some indication that he had been here, openly and honestly. As the car moved down the driveway, he let a glove fall from the window. "It isn't raining now," he said. He was silent after that until Richard turned off to park. "Go farther in. If some gregarious idiot comes along and sees a car, he might get the idea of coming up himself and spoil everything."

"Not much danger of that. Sensible people are all indoors. Not another car on the road."

He couldn't talk any more because of climbing. Had there really been a day when he and Celeste had skimmed swiftly up this tortuous way? Did he think of this place always, because he associated it with his sister? And had he chosen it as the site of a murder because as a jealous boy he had longed for her death here? Well, today he was going to do Celeste a favor.

He gained the top, refusing Richard's offer of a final pull upward. There they lay, the river and the sky, and he walked over to the very edge to cling to the railing and stare. He had spoken one truth. He would never come here again.

"Better not go so close to the edge, sir. It's dangerous."

He looked down at the froth the river made on the rocks. "I suppose no one could make that jump and live." He put his hand on the gun in his pocket and spoke loudly into the wind. "Who do you think stole those letters from you, Richard?"

"I don't—— You've talked to Dolores."

"No."

"Then how did you know they were stolen? I didn't tell the police."

"Why not?"

Richard shrugged. "What good would it have done? They hadn't been able to prevent it. How could they catch the thief afterward?"

"You share my lack of confidence in policemen. We've shared so many opinions, you and I."

The young man moistened his lips. "You're behaving strangely today."

"Because a strange thing has happened to me. Someone mailed me the letters you had received from my niece. Among those letters I found a most interesting paper."

"What sort of paper? I don't remember a——"

"This paper." With his left hand he took out the copy he had made and held it out. "Take it. Look at it. Think how foolish and vain you were to save it."

Richard's bewilderment was magnificent. "What's this supposed to be?"

"It's the paper you tore from Felicia Waring's purse. The paper she was going to return to Dolores along with the news that the

186

glorious lover, depicted therein, had fathered Felicia's child."

"You're crazy! If that's what this is, then you're the one who's guilty. Otherwise, you'd have shown it to the police. I never saw this thing before in my life."

The wind sighed softly and the rain began in earnest. Canby spoke. "Felicia wanted to marry you, and you wanted to marry Dolores. Afterward, I suspect because your mother sensed what you had done, you went to California. But there was no girl there so wealthy and malleable as Dolores. And your parents died. So you were free to come back and try again. Perhaps you saw Howell and recognized him as Harper. Perhaps, prompted by my idle chatter, you went to see Constance Ward and recognized her too. You were frightened. Why were these two here? Somehow they had come to suspect you, they were after you. Was it my name you gave the poor girl to gain admittance to her rooms? I suppose it was. I had told you of that appointment myself."

Richard took a step away from the railing. "You're forgetting something. You say this paper just came into your hands. If that's true, where did it come from? Not from me. I didn't mail you those letters. Whoever did, had the chance to enclose this paper with them." He came closer, smiling. "Don't you see? If Harper stole the letters, then he's the one who——"

Canby drew the gun, held it steady. "It won't do, Richard. Harper could have had no interest in that paper, ever. You mustn't hope for stupidity from me. Every line, every crease, shows that it had lain right where it was, among the letters, for a long time."

The handsome young man looked at the gun and laughed. With precise fingers he tore the paper into small pieces and gave them to the wind. "You're right, Canby. I should have done that long ago." He looked down contemptuously at the little man. "What do you intend to do about it?"

He was proud of the steadiness of his voice. "Because I once found you good company and because Dolores thinks of you as a friend, I'm going to save you from the horror of being executed by the state." He nodded toward the railing. "A quick, clean death. More than you deserve."

"You've thought of everything," said Richard admiringly. "Or

187

nearly." His hand lashed out suddenly, wrested the gun away with one powerful jerk. "Like taking candy from a baby," he said.

Canby looked down at his empty hand. "That will do you no real good. What you destroyed was a copy. The original document is locked in my desk. I am going, now, to give it to Inspector Davis."

"Really? I can't let you do that." He swung his arm and the gun flew in a great arc toward the river. He walked over to Canby, still smiling. "I'm glad you told me where the paper was. There's nothing left for us to discuss." He glanced at the railing. "A quick, clean death, as you said. The gossips will be sorry for you. 'Poor man, he had nothing to live for, neither chick nor child.' But Dolores and I will think of you often and bless you for all you've done for us."

Odd that one's mind could work rapidly when one's body could not move nor one's throat make a sound. He thought of Celeste and her daughter, of the glove he had dropped, of all the high-handed mistakes he had made. Then, as the relentless arms lifted him toward the railing, he saw two men break from the trees and come pounding across the stones, and he found his voice. "Help!" he screamed. "Help!"

He lay where he had been dropped, and the feet rushed past him. He heard a high, thin cry, fading away, and, when he looked up, there were only the two policemen standing by the railing.

O'Brien spoke first. "I didn't think he'd have the nerve. What a hell of a way to die!"

Inspector Davis pocketed his gun. "He earned it," he said.

Then they turned and helped Winthrop Canby to his feet.

Between the tragedy at the Point and traintime at nine that night there was so much excitement and shaking hands and recapitulation that the inspector was worn out. He didn't mind, because, during the commotion, he was a witness to several scenes that pleased him immoderately. One was of Dolores, flushed into beauty, holding out both her hands to him.

"Oh, I wish you could talk to James, but he fell asleep the minute he heard that it was all over. I'll thank you for him. Unless you can stay over until tomorrow, when he'll be able to do it himself. Please stay."

"I can't," he said. "I wish I could."

"We moved him upstairs this afternoon, and the poor darling's exhausted. He'll hate to have missed you."

"He ought to be too happy to care about anything."

"He's a different man—you wouldn't recognize him. He looks so much younger and he behaves—well, he's perfect." She gave a little exclamation and turned to a tray of cocktails. "Mother said I had time to give you a drink before you went to her house for dinner. Martini?"

"Thank you. Aren't you dining with us?"

"No. James might need me."

She sat on an ottoman by his knees and looked like a lovely, confiding child. "It must have been hard on James, my resembling her. Because she hadn't been faithful, he kept expecting me not to be. Burned child dreading the fire, you know. He told me that much, after we'd heard——"

"It was a shock to you, finding out that it was Richard."

"Yes. But, you see, I'd been thinking it was James, and that was much worse. I can't help feeling sad, of course. Whatever Richard was, he was always sweet to me. It wasn't just a question of my money, he wasn't all bad."

"That's right. Felicia had money, too, but he didn't want her. He wanted you."

"Was she on her way to see me at Stone Oaks, when he——"

"Yes." She lowered her head, and he made his voice loudly cheerful. "Well, there are a lot of things about it we'll never know. Did your husband say anything else? Did he tell you where he was the night Felicia died?"

"No, but I know. He must have seen me at the station and followed me to New York. I saw him that night, running down those stairs. I'm sure now it must have been James."

"Down what stairs?" asked the inspector firmly.

"I've forgotten," she said sweetly. "Let me pour you another drink."

Well, there were rewards to this wretched profession he had

189

chosen. The happiness on this girl's face. The knowledge that her husband could sleep peacefully at last. And at the Kennedys' dinner table there were Mr. Kennedy's delighted hospitality and his wife's proud beaming at her animated and tireless brother.

"How did you dare to threaten him, Winthrop? To go up to that lonesome place with him, when you *knew*—— It's the bravest thing I ever heard of!"

"Not at all," said Winthrop magnificently. He turned to the inspector. "I didn't know there had been an ax in James's car. Did Richard put it there?"

"He must have."

"What did he hope to gain by it?"

(Letty came in and beckoned to Mrs. Kennedy. "Miss Dolores on the phone," she said.)

"There's no knowing. Did he intend to come back and put bloodstains on it? Did he want Mrs. Howell to see it there and be suspicious? Was it a warning to James? Your guess is as good as mine."

Canby shook a finger at him. "What stopped him was your being around. It was inspired of Dolores to send for you, and I'll never forgive her for keeping it a secret from me."

Mrs. Kennedy returned, laughing. "James is awake and Dolores wanted to know if I didn't think a mustard plaster would be good for him. I told her absolutely not!"

"You probably saved his life," said Mr. Kennedy. "A mustard plaster ought to be made by somebody who's seen one before."

"Love and mustard plasters," said Winthrop sotto voce to the inspector. "Can you imagine a beautiful and exciting girl settling for that?"

"That's what most of them *do* settle for. Normal procedure."

"Quite right. Revolting, nevertheless. Normality usually is."

Mr. Canby was staying, so the inspector went out to the car with his host, who was to drive him to the station. The weather had cleared and the first stars were showing in a sky that had not forgotten the sunset.

"A fine night," said Mr. Kennedy, opening the car doors.

"Everything smells good after a rain. The sweet alyssum and the nicotiana——"

The inspector drew a deep breath of the fragrant air and thought what a good place the world was when there was time to notice it. The Howell house was entirely dark except for the lighted square of Dolores's bedroom window, and that was fine too. He'd have a great deal to tell Kathryn when he saw her. Did she know about these flowers that smelled so sweet after a rain?

He took out his notebook. "Give me those names again. Nicotiana——"

"And sweet alyssum. They're nothing special. Just very common flowers."

He slipped his notebook back into his pocket and got into the car. "I want to mention them to a friend of mine," he said.